WANT AN EPIC BONUS EPILOGUE FROM THE HOLLINGSWORTHS?

Make sure you sign up for The List at the end of this book, and we'll send it to you. Not only will you get your epilogue, but also access to our no-spam newsletter including exclusive news and updates, sneak peaks at the latest book, and giveaways just for The List.

BREAK

GRAHAME CLAIRE

Break (Bend & Break Duet, Book Two) Grahame Claire

Copyright © 2021 Grahame Claire

All rights reserved. No part of this book can be reproduced in any form or by electronic or mechanical means including information storage and retrieval systems, without the express written permission of the author. The only exception is by a reviewer who may quote short excerpts in a review.

This is a work of fiction. Names, characters, places, and incidents either are the products of the author's imagination or are used fictitiously. Any resemblance to actual persons, living or dead, businesses, companies, events, or locales is entirely coincidental.

Editing And Proofreading:

Marion Archer, Marion Making Manuscripts

Karen Lawson and Janet Hitchcock, The Proof is in the Reading

Lori Sabin

ISBN: 978-1-951878-20-7

For those who break through the hard stuff.

CHAPTER ONE
CAL

"WILL YOU MARRY ME?"

I swerved.

She clutched my thigh as I got the truck back into my lane.

Thank God no one was beside us.

She looked at me expectantly.

My heart beat out of my chest.

I had to pull over or we were going to wreck.

Marry Beau? Marry? Beau?

I sped a few blocks before finding an open spot on the curb.

"Beau . . ." I took off my seat belt to get some relief from the pressure in my chest, but it didn't help.

Her fingers dug into my leg like my answer was the most important thing in the world.

I didn't want her to marry that woman beater, Alex Davenport, but she was desperate.

"Why did you stop? We need to go to Connecticut."

I scrubbed my forehead. "Why are we going to Connecticut?"

"There's no waiting period after we get our marriage license. We can do this today."

What? Today?

"Um . . . that seems impulsive."

If she took a step back, she'd realize being shackled to me wasn't the solution.

"I'll pay off your debt."

"The hell you will," I said, my voice rising. The shock was quickly overpowered by anger. "I don't need your money."

"I have so much it doesn't matter," she said insistently.

Must be nice to never worry about where each dollar went.

"I. Don't. Need. Your. Money."

The truth was, I could use it. But I wouldn't. I'd made financial choices that I had to live with. Ones that I'd take care of. Not her.

"I just wanted to give you something too. So this deal isn't one-sided," she said quietly.

Stab. Stab. Stab.

Deal. Like a business deal.

"So what's the grand plan here? Other than you wouldn't have to marry that other son of a bitch."

"I think if we get married, maybe I can keep my father from doing something to you."

"You just said a second ago we can't stop him." I yanked on my hair.

"I have to try."

Something about the smallness of her voice caused a fissure in my anger.

"You don't even live in this country."

"All the better, right? You can do what you want."

She hadn't grown up with an example of what marriage should be. And in her world, marriages were obviously used as transactions.

But in mine, marriage was sacred.

Ma was still devoted to Dad even though he'd been gone six years. My brothers loved their wives. My grandparents had been devoted, no matter that they bickered like they had been born to argue.

Your brother's wife cheated on him with his best friend and got knocked up.

Well, it was supposed to be sacred.

"I don't want to be married to someone who lives on the other side of the world."

Her face brightened. "If that's a deal breaker, I'll move back. Now can we go to Connecticut?"

"I didn't say yes."

In my wildest imagination, I never pictured a woman asking *me* to marry her. And I sure as hell didn't think that woman would be Beau.

"If you'll just drive, by the time we get there, you'll agree."

In the old days, she was right. *No* wasn't a word I said to her. Ever.

Replacing one groom with another wasn't a solution. I wasn't even sure it was a temporary fix.

Beau was handing me everything I'd ever wanted.

Except she didn't want to spend the rest of her life with me. I was just an easy target.

"I'm sorry, baby sister. But I can't do it."

Her shoulders drooped. I couldn't stand the defeat in her posture, but she'd realize I was right.

"I can't marry him," she whispered.

"But that's not a good enough reason for you to marry me."

She dropped her chin to her chest and fiddled with her gold chain. Then she pulled down the visor and flipped open the mirror.

She used her phone as a light to rub the makeup off her jaw.

Every bruise revealed was like a gut punch.

She glared at her reflection, as if she were furious with herself for ever letting that happen.

"It's not your fault."

I hoped she heard me. Believed me.

"But if I walk down that aisle, when it happens again, it will be."

Damn it.

No. It would be mine. Because she'd asked me to help her. She wouldn't do that again. And next time, it could be broken bones. Violence impossible to hide, given he'd left bruises before they married. And if he raped her?

A marriage license wasn't a right to her body, but I doubted Alex Davenport cared about that.

The image of her screaming, trying to fight him off, clawed at me.

You can stop it. You can make sure he never touches her again. And not just by breaking every bone in his hand.

"How long does it take to get to Connecticut?"

CHAPTER TWO

BEAU

MY HAND SHOOK as I signed the marriage license.

Cal saw it.

And I couldn't stand that he'd seen yet another moment of my weakness. As much as I wanted to claim it was anger that shuddered through my body because I was forced to get married, even if wasn't to my father's pick, I couldn't. I *was* mad. But these were straight-up nerves.

The jolt of pain through my arm was a reminder of why I had to do this. I didn't want to marry Cal, and he didn't want to marry me. At least this way, I wasn't losing control of my life. I was choosing Cal.

He may have caused me emotional hurt many years ago, but he'd never hurt me physically. I hoped we could find a way to cohabitate where we were nothing more than roommates until we could untangle ourselves.

Damn it. We had no prenup. And there wasn't time. But between spending one second with Alex as his wife or giving up at least half of what I had to Cal to keep that from happening . . . I'd gladly give it all to Cal. Gladly might be a bit strong, but the alternative was far worse.

When I passed the paper to Cal, I hadn't regained control of my physical reaction. To make matters worse, he felt my fingers tremble when he took the pen. He signed his name confidently. Because nothing rattled him. Nothing.

He was meant to be a fireman. Not many people could face danger without blinking.

And I didn't know anyone who could run on as little sleep and still look devastating.

I hated I noticed how his muscles stretched his long-sleeved T-shirt. How his jeans hung low on his hips in just the right way. How he probably hadn't brushed his dark hair in a day and it looked perfectly mussed.

I hated how I pressed my legs together, knowing just how that stubble felt against my thighs. How after everything we'd been through, I couldn't turn off the physical desire I had for him.

"Congratulations." The official gave Cal the completed marriage license. "May you have a lifetime of happiness."

I just wanted to survive.

And that made me angry all over again. Maybe my life hadn't been my own, but I'd made the most of it. This was like trying to be shoved into a box that was welded shut.

"We have about an hour before our appointment with the minister. Want something to eat?" Cal asked as we stepped outside of the courthouse.

He'd insisted a person in some religious capacity perform the ceremony. Why, I didn't know. He really was unflappable, taking a sacred oath before God that was a lie.

I wasn't in a position to argue, so I'd found someone willing to do it on the fly.

"I'm not hungry."

Could he eat now? My stomach was in knots. This wasn't even real, but my nerves were jittering like it was.

He held open the car door, and even what was once the safest place in the world couldn't settle me.

When he got in, the unsettledness became worse.

He draped his arms over the steering wheel, but didn't crank the truck. "I don't have another shirt." He glanced down, his tone almost apologetic.

I had on jeans and a sweater. It wasn't exactly wedding attire. Except Pepper wanted to get married just like this. But she was with my brother for love. Clothes didn't matter.

When we weren't getting married for love, they didn't matter either. "It's fine."

"Those shops probably don't open for a while," he said as if he hadn't heard me.

"This is just a formality. We don't have to be dressed to the nines." I sunk down in the seat. Had it even been two minutes since we'd gotten back in the car? How was I going to make it an hour?

"Seems disrespectful," he continued.

"Should I call my father and have him deliver the dress he picked out for me to wear for Alex?" I snapped. *Just an hour, Beau. You can make it an hour.*

He balled his fingers. "No."

I cocked my head. "Isn't it *disrespectful* to use someone for her virginity?" *Shut up, Beau. He is your only ticket out. And you're showing just how hurt you still are that he dumped you. Get a backbone.*

I used to have one. Then I'd been summoned back to New York, thought I could dance with the devil, and all the old feelings I thought I'd dealt with came crashing back with a vengeance.

He didn't have the decency to look at me. Those dark eyes stared straight out the windshield, and I had no idea what was going on in that thick skull of his.

"You sure I'm your guy for this?" he finally asked.

"I'm not exactly swimming in options." I folded my arms.

"Still a last resort for you," he muttered.

"What does that mean?" I asked, sniffling bitterly.

"Nothing."

I twisted in my seat. "It sounds like something."

An argument could make the time go faster and *that* was something we excelled at.

"Back then . . ." He couldn't say when we were together, and that just irritated me even more. "You wouldn't have chosen me if there were other options."

I gaped at him. What?

"*I did choose you*," I cried.

Cal had always been the most confident man I knew. To hear his insecurities . . . threw me further off balance.

"You wanted the forbidden," he said evenly. "You liked seeing how far you could take it without getting caught." His gaze was cold when he turned it on me. "This is still a game to you. Daddy's gonna be real pissed you married me, isn't he?"

I opened my mouth and closed it, stunned into silence. Yes, my father was going to be furious, but that didn't have a damn thing to do with why I was marrying Cal.

And was that really how he saw me? That I'd used him as some sort of forbidden fruit to get my kicks?

I wouldn't dignify him with an answer.

"This was a terrible idea," I muttered. "Just go back to New York. I'll figure something out."

He waved the marriage certificate in front of my face. "Oh no, baby sister. This says we're partners for life. And I didn't just drive all the way to Connecticut for nothing. We're getting married."

"Don't act like Connecticut is across the country." I glared.

He glared back. "If I don't leave this state as your husband, it might as well be."

"Stop pretending you want this."

"I'd be better off marrying a mountain lion, but I'll be damned if I let that son of a bitch ever lay another finger on you."

My heart squeezed at the same time I felt a fist to the gut. Cal was doing one of the kindest things anyone had ever done for me. He was protecting me. But it hurt that being married to me was so repulsive to him.

Why did I care?

This was just a business transaction.

Except we had no agreement. I was the only one benefiting. And if

Cal would do this for me, expecting nothing in return, that meant there was something decent in him.

And if there was something decent in him, maybe I'd been wrong to hate him so much.

He's not that man from years ago. I'd experienced how decent he could be in the way he cared for me—sheltered me—after Alex assaulted me.

Anger had kept me strong and shielded for so many years. And to defeat my father, to stay on this new trajectory, I had to cling to my anger like a lifeline.

He shoved open the door. "Let's go see if we can get this over with."

CHAPTER THREE

CAL

"YOU'RE EARLY. It's lovely to see a couple so eager to begin their journey together."

I didn't bother to tell the old man we'd started this trip a long time ago and it was destined for hell.

Wordlessly, Beau followed him into the chapel. Ma would kill me if she knew I'd set foot in a church dressed like this.

She wouldn't kill you for getting married without telling her?

That was probably a worse offense, but I wasn't sure she'd ever know. I was at Beau's mercy. This was her show and I was just along for the ride. Like always.

You could've protested harder.

Maybe. It would've been the smart thing to do for both of us. We were good at hurting each other. But this had seemed the most logical solution to her massive problem.

And maybe the fastest one to yours too.

And even though I'd needed to let go of her—to move on and go back to life as I'd been living since she left—the idiotic part of me grasped this harebrained idea like it was pure genius.

I didn't believe some vows and a legal document would change anything between us. It probably complicated things.

But I wanted to make it harder to walk away. What had surprised me was her outburst in the car. God, I was sorry that she'd been so hurt by my actions—choices I'd made to ensure she found the happy future she deserved.

Now that I'd had a minute to think on it, that surprised the hell out of me. Beau didn't need me. She didn't let anything get to her. Look at how fast she'd come up with a solution to her marriage problem.

But if I still affected her after all these years, what did that mean?

Don't even go there, man.

I had no place in her life, not even as a real fake husband. And it wasn't wise to get comfortable in that role.

"Have you prepared your own vows?" the minister asked kindly.

"No."

We both answered at the same time and that seemed to amuse the man.

"Lucky for you, I have some." He held up a black binder and grinned.

It should've been funny, but I couldn't laugh.

A long time ago, on the fire station rooftop with Beau asleep in my arms, I'd let myself have one moment to think about a future with her. There were kids, backyard barbecues with family and friends, and long aimless drives around the city. And so much damn happiness it had made my chest hurt.

Those were the most dangerous thoughts I'd ever had.

Because I couldn't hold on to something that had never belonged to me.

And the next day, I'd let her go.

I never imagined a wedding, but if I had, it wouldn't have been like this.

"Join hands, please."

She looked at mine like they were vats of acid. I took her delicate hands in my rough ones before she decided to run. Even our hands were opposites. Hers were soft and smooth. Mine were cut and calloused. But they fit together like puzzle pieces.

The minister spoke, but he might as well have been a million miles away. It sounded like he was in a barrel. Or maybe I was.

I couldn't look at Beau.

This whole charade was for her benefit. I should be able to find some peace, knowing I'd be able to keep her safe.

But I couldn't.

She wasn't marrying me because she wanted to. She was doing it because she *had* to.

Stab. Stab. Stab. Stab.

That shouldn't matter. But I hated the lie with everything in me.

Necessary lies were what got us to this point. Where we could hardly stand the sight of one another . . . although our bodies hadn't gotten that message.

And it was too painful to be near her, knowing what I'd given up.

It didn't matter that my intentions were noble and for the best. Standing at this altar with her hands in mine was like a knife hollowing out my chest with jagged swipes.

And I felt every single one of them.

"Do you take this woman to be your lawfully wedded wife?"

The question was a gunshot, nearly knocking me backward. This was it. No going back. Though if I were honest, we'd reached that point when I'd picked her up hours ago. Hell, maybe we'd reached it the second we'd met.

"I do."

The two words sounded as if they were dragged from me. I'd just made a vow and couldn't even look her in the eyes when I did it.

"Do you take this man to be your lawfully wedded husband?"

And then I could no longer look away. Would she go through with this?

She glared at me mournfully as if I'd put her in this position. As if I were the one who'd put those bruises on her jaw.

"I . . ."

What? We'd been up all night. She'd convinced me this was the *only* solution. What was she doing?

"Are you playing with me, Beau?"

"If we skip the rest is it still legal?" She pulled on her hands like holding mine for much longer was too much.

In another time and place, I might have been insulted she didn't want to go through the whole spiel, but I just wanted to get this over with too.

I had to give the minister credit. This had to be the most shocking response, especially for a couple so *eager* to get married. Somehow he kept his features neutral. "Well, no, I need . . . um, consent . . . to legalize the marriage. For you, Beau, to consent to this union. So, do you take this man to be your lawfully wedded husband?"

She lifted her chin in defiance. "Fine. Yes, I do."

The minister shifted uncomfortably. "Okay. I can now pronounce you husband and wife. You may kiss the bride."

She hadn't let me anywhere near her mouth since she'd been back. Like kissing me was too intimate. And I'd been on board with that. Just because these vows had been forced didn't mean I wasn't taking them seriously. Because this was Beau.

And that included sealing our deal the proper way.

I leaned forward.

She pulled her hands out of mine and shoved them against my chest. "Don't even think about it."

But I wouldn't force her into something she didn't want. Especially not after the hell she'd been through lately.

"Mrs. Calhoun," I murmured against her cheek before I kissed the soft skin.

She stiffened but accepted the gesture.

Fake or not. Bad circumstance or real. She might've picked the wrong man to rescue her.

Because I hadn't just said those vows. I meant them.

And I didn't break promises.

Which was going to be a huge problem when she wanted me to let her go.

Because I'd just married the only woman I'd ever loved.

CHAPTER FOUR

BEAU

MRS. CALHOUN.

I'd married Cal. I'd. Married. Cal.

Was I insane?

And what would happen next?

Where was the relief that I couldn't marry Alex now? I was extraordinarily happy about that. And even though I hadn't behaved like it, I was grateful to Cal that he'd saved me from that horror.

But this brought on a whole new problem. I'd acted on impulse. In desperation. And hadn't given a thought beyond the ceremony.

"It's not Bora Bora, but there's a diner in Woodlawn that has a killer breakfast."

I inched closer to the car door like a child instead of a woman who could handle herself. "Why would we go there? To celebrate?" I asked crisply.

"To eat. I'm starved," he said with a smirk. "But I'd think you'd want to celebrate. You got what you wanted, right?"

My stomach knotted.

Yes. I had gotten what I wanted.

No.

I was married to Cal. And I didn't want that . . . not like I used to.

I looked across the car at him. We could've done this ten years ago. Would we still be happy? Would we still be doing this? Riding around in his truck? Would we have kids?

I swallowed hard. The thought of being responsible for another human being was terrifying. But he'd come from a big family. And . . . *none of that matters now.*

Part of me mourned the loss of time we'd never get back.

What did I think this was? The start of a happily-ever-after?

He was my fake husband, not my real husband.

And I was lost.

Mrs. Calhoun.

Mrs. Calhoun.

Beau Calhoun.

I'd always been a Hollingsworth. And now I wasn't.

I drew in a deep breath and some weight lifted off of me. Cal hadn't just given me an out from a wedding I didn't want to go through, he'd freed me from the name I hadn't realized was weighing me down.

My only pride in it was because of my brothers.

"You testing out your new name?"

I blinked at Cal. *Had I said it out loud?*

"I didn't realize what a relief it would be to get rid of my last name," I said quietly.

This man had seen me at my most vulnerable. Maybe he didn't deserve my inner thoughts, but I had nothing to hide. Or maybe he did deserve them because he had stepped up for me. Again.

He braked at a red light. "I'm surprised you'd want mine."

The honesty in his words ripped my chest wide open. There was something in them, something raw, that made me ache. Like I felt *his* pain.

"I can't believe I'm saying this, but I'm so glad to have it. I kind of want to skip the diner honeymoon and go change all my identification and credit cards." I slumped down in the seat, feeling lighter.

"You can't officially have my name until we consummate this marriage."

I pressed my thighs together. My body never had gotten the message that I was supposed to avoid this man.

His gaze drifted over to mine. "And we can't consummate this marriage until you're healed."

I swallowed around the knot in my throat. So much of me appreciated that he was thoughtful enough to be careful. And so much of me hated that that alone proved me somewhat wrong about him being so awful.

I'm healed. I'm healed.

But that was the overwhelming desire talking.

We're not consummating anything.

My head chimed in.

As much as I wanted to cut myself off from Cal physically, I wasn't stupid enough to believe I really could. I was the one willing to risk further injury just to feel him cover me with his big body. To take me places no other person ever could.

He was the one who had so easily put the brakes on all physical contact.

Was it really in the name of protection? Or had he already grown tired of me?

He still made it look so easy to walk away. Sure, he was here . . . and my husband . . . but he'd been able to stop touching me like it was nothing.

I still craved him on a level I couldn't comprehend.

He parked the car in front of an old building. "You aren't spitting fire at me. Should I be scared?"

I glared. When had Garrett Calhoun been afraid of anything?

"We consummated this marriage plenty *before* we said I do."

He took off his seat belt. "That was you trying to work me out of your system." That cocky coolness that had possessed me from the first time we met was no less effective now. "Not working out so well now, is it, *Mrs. Calhoun?*"

I shoved open the door. "Are we eating or not?"

I wanted to tell him to stop calling me that but couldn't force the words out of my mouth. Because I liked it. In some ways, I felt like a new person. Like I was starting over.

He stalked around the car and caged me against it. His face was so close to mine, I had to hold my breath so I didn't lose my head. But it was too late. I'd already gotten a hint of whatever it was that made Cal so irresistible.

"You think if you don't kiss me that makes us less intimate? More like strangers?" His demand was a low growl that I felt in my core.

I lifted my chin but still couldn't breathe.

"We aren't strangers, baby sister. Never have been. Never will be." He inched closer until our mouths were only millimeters apart.

"I only kiss people I love." I was surprised my words sounded strong instead of breathless. The way I felt.

Until Alex had taken what wasn't his, that was the truth. I'd only loved one man. Only kissed one man.

And now that man was my husband.

I fisted his shirt with both hands so tightly my hands hurt. Was I trying to keep him in place? Or keep him away?

The weeks since I'd returned to New York flashed through my mind at warp speed. Cal was the one constant, the one person I'd been able to count on. Sure, if I'd been honest with my brothers or Lexie, they would have been too. But when I'd needed to work things out on my own, Cal had been right with me, a steadying force.

I squeezed my eyes shut. The truth slammed down on me and it was too hard to accept. I couldn't face it. Couldn't face him.

"Don't close your eyes." The low rumble vibrated through me.

In the way only Cal could, he soothed me, bolstered my confidence, and terrified me all at once.

On a deep breath, I opened my eyes again.

Those dark pools were intense as they stared back at me. I had no idea what he was thinking, only that I *felt* so so much. More than I wanted to feel. It was as if those vows had ripped off a layer of protection I'd been hiding behind for the longest time. A layer of lies I'd been telling myself.

I no longer hated this man. How could I?

I swallowed hard. This man had sacrificed at least his immediate future for me. And he hadn't hesitated. He came when I called. And there was only one time in our history he hadn't given me what I needed.

But I was beginning to wonder if he thought he had.

"Have you had a good life?" he asked quietly. Tentatively.

"Yes."

"Did you accomplish everything you wanted?"

"Mostly."

"Are you happy?"

"When I'm not in New York, yes. I'm happy."

"Then I didn't make a mistake."

Then I didn't make a mistake.

Now that the layer of lies I'd been telling myself was gone, I could see so much clearer. He'd let me go all those years ago so I would be happy and accomplish everything I'd wanted. Because he'd believed I wouldn't do that if I'd stayed with him. Cal didn't act like a man who was indifferent.

And if he wasn't indifferent . . . what did he feel?

What did *I* feel?

"Thank you," I whispered. Had I said that? I couldn't remember, but regardless of my mixed up emotions, I owed him my gratitude at the very least.

His brow wrinkled ever so slightly. "I didn't do anything." He glanced away.

I turned his face back toward me. "You've done more than I deserve."

He recoiled. "There's nothing I wouldn't do for you," he said gruffly.

Oddly enough, I believed him.

And if it weren't for his body and the truck, I'd have swayed on my feet at the realization.

"We should go have breakfast." The words came out breathless. I didn't want food.

I wanted to burrow into Cal, let him make the world disappear. Make me feel the way only he could.

That scared me.

We'd been married less than three hours.

And I already didn't want to let him go.

CHAPTER FIVE

CAL

"YOU GONNA ANSWER THAT?"

I pointed at her phone. This was the fourth time *Father* had flashed on her screen.

She picked up a piece of bacon and pointed it at me. "Give me your honest opinion."

I blinked at her. I wasn't sure what had happened when I'd had her pinned against my truck outside, but something had.

And it had taken every bit of my human strength not to kiss her.

I craved her mouth, needed it, maybe now more than I needed to be inside her. She'd meant what she said. That she only kissed people she loved. My gut told me she hadn't shared her mouth with many people.

I stamped down the irrational flare of jealousy.

What if she'd only ever kissed me?

She waved the now half-eaten piece of bacon in front of me. "I didn't realize I'd said fighting words."

I snatched the bacon and polished it off.

"Hey! Do you know how long it's been since I've had food like this?" She leaned back in the diner booth. "It's so good, but I think I've overdone it."

"And you're admitting that?"

She used to eat heartily. I didn't like the idea of her not getting the proper nutrition. She'd always been thin, and she still was. But why didn't she eat?

"It's the sugar. And the grease." She looked down at her mostly empty plate. She'd demolished the blueberry pancakes. Actually, it was more like she'd had syrup with a side of pancakes.

"Do they not have good food like this in London?" I pushed my plate away.

"I try to take care of myself." She wiped her mouth with her napkin. "And I know me well enough to realize if I have all the things I'm not supposed to, I can't stop."

Somehow I felt like that applied to me too.

But I didn't mind. Maybe that meant she wouldn't be able to let me go.

"I doubt you wanted my thoughts about proper nutrition." I had plenty of opinions on that, but was sure she didn't want to hear them.

"There are only days until the wedding."

I had the sudden urge to turn over this table and thrash the entire restaurant.

She's your wife.

That eased my temper a fraction. Legally, she was, but that wasn't enough.

"What's smarter?" She continued as if a war weren't taking place in my head. "To keep behaving normally? Or to take charge?"

"Is ignoring your father's phone calls normal?" I inclined my head toward the device, which lit up again.

I couldn't imagine Ma calling me like that under any circumstance unless it was a dire emergency. What did her father do to her? What kind of power did he have over her?

"Not really." Her shoulders slumped.

I couldn't stand that anyone had the ability to diminish her fire.

"What's the end game here?" I was playing blind but had no doubt I was definitely a player.

"Freedom."

The word was spoken so softly, I almost didn't hear it. I reached for her hand. My instinct had always been to protect her. Always. And now, it had just ramped up another notch.

I'd had one conversation with her father and understood her fear. Power radiated from him. But I intended to have another one with him and soon. What he'd allowed to happen to Beau—to *my wife*—was unacceptable.

Gently, I squeezed her uninjured fingers. "It's yours. Take it."

"It's not that simple," she whispered. "I have to be smart. He's always five steps ahead."

Had she lived with this fear all her life? As I dug through memories from long ago, I realized that yes, she had been scared of him back then too.

She was mine now. Even if it was only temporary. And I'd protect her with everything I had.

"Stop playing his game."

She gaped at me.

"You don't understand—"

"You're the bravest, strongest person I've ever met. And I know he terrifies you. I *understand* that he's more than willing to give you away to a wife beater. I *understand* that ain't normal." I pointed to her phone, which was lit again with his name. "I think I've got a pretty firm grasp of what's going on here."

She drew in a long breath. When her eyes met mine, they were so haunted it sent a chill racing down my spine. "You have no idea." She spoke so quietly, I wasn't sure if she didn't want me to hear or was afraid he would, wherever he was.

And then it was like she'd been jolted. She waved our server down and shoved cash in her palm before grabbing her phone and sliding out of the booth.

"Did you just pay for our wedding breakfast?" I asked as I trailed her out of the diner.

"Who cares," she said over her shoulder.

I held open the door—barely, since she'd shoved it wide before I could get there.

"You don't have to be a gentleman," she said as I unlocked her side of the truck. That door, I did hold.

"My ma would kill me if I didn't." Damn. She was going to be heartbroken I'd gotten married without her being there. Without her knowing.

Beau furrowed her brow. "What's wrong?"

"I just realized Ma's going to be upset I got married without her." She needed any kind of joy she could find. And she'd been after me to bring a nice girl home. She'd love Beau.

She touched my chest. "We could do it again, if you want. A family ceremony?"

"You'd marry me again?" I asked incredulously. The first time had seemed hard enough on her.

"We're going to have to stay this way for . . . a while." She looked at me almost apologetically.

I hated that.

I wasn't sorry we were married. The longer she was my wife, the more used to it I became. Sorry wouldn't even begin to cover what I'd feel when I had to let her go.

I nodded. Words lodged in my throat as I took her in. We'd been up all night, but she was still the most beautiful thing that had ever walked this earth.

And she was my wife.

That knowledge gave me little comfort, though part of me held on to it with an iron grip. It was temporary. She hadn't married me because she couldn't live without me. I was her only option. That stung. But I wouldn't get mixed up in my feelings.

Beau needed my help.

I could do that.

All I'd ever done was make sure she had what was best for her.

"Where to? Lincoln's to get your things?" I asked as I got into the driver's seat.

"Take me to the office," she said when I cranked the engine. "I have to go to my father's, and I don't want to put you in a more precarious position than I already have."

I froze with my hand on the gear shift. "You aren't going anywhere near him."

She whipped her head toward me. "He's forced me to stay there—"

"Define forced."

"He sent his butler to Lincoln's apartment to collect my belongings and escort me out."

Anger started as a vigorous tingle beneath my skin. "And you didn't want to go?" I asked carefully, just to make sure I heard right.

"No."

That tingle rattled into a violent shake.

"If you think I'm taking you back to him, think again," I growled.

She belonged to me now. I didn't want to control her. But it was my duty to protect her.

"All of my things are there."

"Leave them. You can always get new stuff."

She fidgeted with the gold chain as if weighing her options.

"Or if you really want your things, I'll go get them."

Her eyes flared. "No. We have to be smart, Cal."

"You already said that." My hand was still wrapped tight around the gear shift as a war raged inside of me. That visit to her father had just bumped itself up the list another few spots . . . to the top.

She rolled the chain between her thumb and index finger. Then she dropped her chin to her chest. "I don't know what to do. I've created such a mess."

I reached for her hand and took her soft fingers in mine. Somehow, she'd always had the power to soothe me with her touch. I was supposed to be a balm to her, but she had turned my fury down to a simmer by letting me hold her hand.

"Look at me." I waited until she lifted those dark eyes. "Whether you meant to or not, you just picked your teammate. And baby sister, we aren't going to lose."

CHAPTER SIX

BEAU

HOW COULD he be so confident?

Because he has no idea what we're up against.

But part of me believed him. When I was with Cal, I felt safe yet anything but, all at once. I didn't understand the ferocity of his protectiveness, but it had seeped into my bones.

I couldn't believe I'd admitted to him I didn't know what I was doing. Somehow, it was a relief to unburden that. I was tired of trying so hard to appear in control and put together. Even if he was the last person I wanted to see my weakness, he'd helped me.

And he hadn't judged.

Teammate.

Something must have happened when we'd spoken our vows because suddenly that wasn't such an abhorrent thought. I hadn't worked through the day-to-day schematics of a marriage with him. I supposed somewhere deep down I figured we'd keep our lives separate.

He'd do his thing, and I'd do mine.

I didn't want to go back to the haunted prison I'd grown up in. Cal refusing to let me hadn't made me angry and defensive like I thought it would. He'd relieved yet another valve of pressure I hadn't realized was near bursting.

And he hadn't let go of my hand.

I drew strength from that touch. It was dangerous to need him. This had an expiration date. I'd already survived him leaving me once. As much as I didn't want to admit it, not even to myself . . . I did need Cal.

"In my head, I picture that extravagant circus they're putting on. All those people at the church. And the embarrassment for all of them when I don't show up at the altar." I leaned my head back against the seat. It would be the ultimate vengeance to humiliate all of them—especially my father—in front of their social circle.

"If that's what you want, do it."

Cal made everything simple. Like there was an option A or B. Yes or no. There was no gray area or blurred lines.

"Then I have to act as I have been for another three days."

"You mean living and working with that asshole?" He looked at me. "Ain't happening."

That was the moment I was supposed to not so politely remind him that he couldn't tell me what to do. But it felt so good having someone stand up for me, I didn't want to.

If I'd told my brothers what was going on, they would have been right there for me every step of the way. But I couldn't burden them—damn it. My brothers.

What would father do to them?

"I have to. He's threatened Pepper and Lexie if I don't fall in line." My eyes stung. "And your family."

"Have you talked to Lincoln and Teague about this?" he asked gruffly. He didn't seem to feel any of the fear I did.

"No. They've both waited so long to be happy. And they've always protected me. It's my turn to do that for them."

What was it about Cal that made me unleash everything I'd been holding in?

He made a noncommittal noise. "I get that. I do the same thing with my family. But if your father is as formidable an opponent as you say he is, we need everybody working together."

He was right. But I didn't want to hear it.

"What if something happens to Lexie or Pepper? What if, by telling your brothers, it could be prevented? Is it better to keep your mouth shut?"

I scowled. "You really have a way of putting things in perspective."

"I'd want you to tell me the same thing." He squeezed my fingers. "Call your brothers. My pop used to call these things a get-together."

"What am I going to do? Invite them to dinner?"

He glanced in the rearview mirror. "If that black car following us is who I think it is, we don't have until dinner."

I twisted around. Bile rose up my throat.

He'd found us.

Or maybe he was just following Cal. Either option was unacceptable.

My hand shook as I dialed.

"Where are you?"

"Well, good morning to you too." Something about the normalcy with Lincoln eased my tension a fraction.

"Dad just called me, incredibly unhappy that I was unaware of your whereabouts." Underneath that terseness was worry.

"I'm sorry I put that on you," I said softly. "I need to see you. Teague too. Somewhere safe. We can't keep living like this."

"Let me secure a location. I'll call you back in five minutes."

He was gone before I could agree.

I looked behind us. The car was still there. "How are we going to lose them?"

"Leave that to me. You just call Teague."

He was the more easygoing brother, but in some ways, he was even more protective than Lincoln. And I was more nervous about talking to him.

But he was my brother.

My friend.

"Hey." It wasn't Teague's voice that answered his phone. "He's in the shower."

"Are you his receptionist now?" A smile cracked my lips.

"I was hoping to guilt trip you into coming over. There are some puppies who'd like to see you." Pepper was quiet a second. "And some people too."

I wanted to hug her. "That's what I was calling about."

"Perfect. I can't promise you won't get grilled about"—she lowered her voice—"you know who. But I can talk about our wedding plans a lot if it will help."

She hated wedding planning and the fact she was willing to do that made me love my almost sister-in-law even more.

"I don't have to answer anything he asks," I said, even though that wasn't exactly true. With my fragile emotional state, I'd cave.

"I didn't mean Teague would grill you. I meant Miss Adeline."

A laugh burst from my throat. "There's no getting out of that."

"Afraid not."

"Who are you talking to?" Teague's voice was muffled in the background.

"Your sister."

There was a rustling noise. "Why didn't you tell me?"

Guilt swamped over me in a tidal wave. I tried to push it aside. "Are you answering the phone like your brother now?" My attempt at sounding normal came off strained.

"And you're still not going to," he muttered.

"I need to see you," I said. "Lincoln is supposed to call me back . . . actually he's calling now. Hang on."

I switched the line to Lincoln. "I'm talking to Teague. Let me connect all of us." I pressed a few buttons on my phone. "Everyone there?"

"I'm here."

"Here."

"Daniel has agreed to let us meet at his apartment. Can you be there in thirty minutes?"

"I can be there in about two," Teague said since he lived in the same building. "What the hell is going on?"

"I'll see you both soon." This time I hung up first.

I slumped in my seat.

"You're doing the right thing."

I wasn't sure of that, but it was too late to turn back now. "Go to Teague's."

He switched lanes and flipped on a turn signal. "Totally your call, but you should tell them about . . ." Ever so gently he swiped his finger along my jaw.

It was as if it were too painful for him to speak about what Alex had done to me.

"They'll kill him."

"No, I'm going to."

I jerked my head toward him. He sounded serious. And while I wouldn't mind a lot of bodily harm coming to Alex, I didn't want Cal to suffer the consequences. Without a shadow of doubt, my father would go after everything to do with Cal's family. They'd be destroyed.

"Cal . . ."

He gripped the steering wheel. "Don't call me that."

"Everyone else does."

He stopped at a light, his gaze intense when he looked at me. "And you're not everyone else."

We were back at that first time we met, when we'd said those words to each other. They were true then and they were true now. Except he wasn't just anyone either. Something in me had recognized that before my brain had. Because he was Garrett. My Garrett.

"I'm not telling them we're married."

His jaw worked. "Your show. How are you gonna explain why I'm with you?"

I swallowed hard. "We're . . . together?" Why was that so hard to get out? He was my husband. It didn't get more *together* than that.

But he wasn't mine.

And why hadn't I told him I was talking to my brothers alone?

Because you want him there.

I did.

I wasn't afraid to face my brothers. They loved me no matter how many mistakes I made. But Cal had seen me through these past difficult weeks. Maybe they didn't need to know the extent, but he deserved credit.

And it would be nice to have someone behind me.

He was confident in everything he did. Even driving the truck, he was in command, always knew what to do. Was that what had always drawn me to him?

Often, I felt reckless. Like I was spiraling out of control. Like nothing was my decision.

When I was with Cal, I didn't worry about anything . . . except getting hurt again.

"Why haven't you moved on?" I asked quietly.

I thought I knew why I hadn't. I didn't want to go through the pain again. Not to mention, he still had pieces of my heart. But I was beginning to wonder if it was more than risking my feelings again. If it was because no one else was Cal.

"Moved on?" His brow furrowed.

"Why aren't you married with a nagging wife and a brood of kids?" It hurt to say the words. To think about him with another life. But family meant everything to him. He thrived on it.

He stared straight ahead. "Who was I gonna move on to? There is no one better than you."

CHAPTER SEVEN

CAL

I HAD nothing to lose but her.

I was supposed to keep my distance. Supposed to pretend like I didn't care so she could have the best in life. Live how she wanted to.

What I wanted wasn't important.

She came first. Always had.

And she deserved a hell of a lot more than a man like me.

But she was mine for however long that might be.

Apparently, my head had forgotten I was supposed to hold back. Admitting there was no one better than Beau? Something in me wanted her to know I felt that way. That she was more than good enough for me. Too good for me. And I hated I'd ever made her feel anything less than that.

We stood in opposite corners of the opulent elevator.

This was her world. Filled with gold and jewels and more money than would fit in a Brinks truck.

I was jeans and T-shirts and broke.

I had nothing to give her other than my unwavering support.

She fiddled with that damn necklace.

She needs you, Cal. Not your distance.

I'd made a vow to her. Even if it was temporary, it meant something to me.

I stretched out my arm. She looked at it warily, with vulnerability I didn't like. I preferred her confidence. I hated anything or anyone that made her doubt herself.

Instead of taking my hand, she slid against me, molding her body to my side. I wrapped my arm around her and kissed the top of her head, praying I could take away some of her worry.

There was a time not so long ago, maybe even a few hours ago, she wouldn't have let me hold her on the principle of it. I couldn't believe her warmth was against me now.

While I wasn't particularly looking forward to a showdown with her brothers, I drew strength from her. Would it be enough when she went back to London and left me behind?

Focus on the here and now.

It was selfish, but I would. There was a shitstorm outside of this elevator, but for one brief moment, we had calm. And I'd take it.

There was a polite chime and the elevator slowed to a smooth stop. The doors slid back, revealing a foyer that probably cost more than Ma's house.

Beau untucked herself from my side, and I immediately felt the loss. She curled her fingers around my bicep and led us toward massive double doors to what I assumed was an apartment.

They both flew open and a woman with dark hair grabbed both of our hands, dragging us inside.

I stumbled forward. This wasn't the greeting I expected. I thought rich people were supposed to be stuffy and formal.

"Beau." The woman pulled her in for a bear hug. "Should've known I could count on you to bring lots of gorgeous men to our apartment."

My face got hot.

Beau snickered. "I'm good for something," she said lightly. How did she manage to put on a brave face with so much chaos going on? "Vivian, this is Garrett Calhoun. Cal, this is Vivian Elliott."

"Nice to meet you," I said awkwardly.

"Likewise." She motioned us forward. "Come on. They're all in Daniel's study."

I tried to keep my wide-eyed stare to a minimum, but this place was... crazy nice.

"I'm not going to hold it against you that you haven't been by to see us." Vivian winked at Beau. "Looks like you've been occupied. But now, neither of you have an excuse not to come over for dinner."

What?

I didn't know this woman, but she was already extending an invite? I didn't belong in their world. But she had on an old pair of holey jeans, a faded sweatshirt, and ballet shoes. She hadn't even balked at my worn boots on her expensive floors.

"What is *he* doing here?" Teague thrust his finger in my direction. Not so long ago, I would've gotten a much friendlier greeting. Yeah, that stung. But it was more expected than Vivian's warm welcome.

Beau breezed into the study as if she'd been there a million times before. She kissed both cheeks of a man I didn't know. He towered over her and reminded me a lot of Lincoln.

"Daniel, thank you for letting us invade your home on such short notice." She gave him a warm smile.

"You're always welcome."

"Except I think I'm close to pissing off that one for not coming over for dinner." She pointed her head in Vivian's direction.

"I don't recommend doing that." His gaze landed on the woman with a flash of tenderness before it roved to me. "I don't believe we've met."

"And I don't believe you have any business being here," Teague said, glaring.

"Garrett Calhoun. Call me Cal," I extended a hand.

He grasped my hand and shook. "Daniel Elliott."

"Chill out, Teague," Beau said.

"I thought you hated him."

"That's our cue to leave you to it. If you need us, we'll be in the kitchen," Daniel said.

"Actually, I'll be eavesdropping right outside," Vivian corrected with a grin. "This sounds interesting." She practically skipped from the room with her husband right behind.

I stared at the empty space near the doorway, feeling a bit blindsided. These people weren't what I expected at all, though I hadn't given much thought to what we'd face once here.

Lincoln hadn't said a word since our arrival, but his sharp gaze assessed everything. He studied Beau and me. Somehow that was more unnerving than Teague's blunt hostility. It was as if Lincoln had an invisible hold around my neck, squeezing with increasing pressure as he determined just how much I'd hurt Beau.

She marched over to where they stood without hesitation. There was no doubt who was truly in charge of this family. And it wasn't the men.

That reminded me of my ma. She was the queen and her six sons were her subjects. Just like our pa had taught us.

"Our problems are so much bigger than my relationship status." She pointed to the chairs in front of the desk and motioned for them to sit.

They did.

"I thought your relationship status was engaged," Teague grumbled.

She gave me a knowing look. The status was married. And I loved that secret smile that played on her lips. She motioned for me to join her where she was propped against the desk.

I obeyed without thought.

"I want both of you to promise to keep your cool," she said.

It was so easy to picture her leading her company just like this. She was in charge, leaving no room for doubt or fear.

"Seeing how this has started, I don't think I can make that promise," Teague said.

She bent and touched his knee. "Try. You're the bravest out of the three of us. And we need your courage."

If her words upset Lincoln, he didn't show it. Although I wasn't sure his expression would change if a leprechaun pranced into the room.

Somehow, her words seemed to smooth Teague's temper.

"I'm not marrying Alex Davenport. I'm being forced to stay at Father's against my will. And if I don't keep in line, he's threatened to do something to Lexie and Pepper."

She ripped the Band-Aid off instead of tiptoeing around. Would she have been so direct if we'd been together all this time?

You didn't mow the yard. Your forgot to pick up milk. And I want a kiss.

I pressed my lips together to keep from smiling. It was a completely inappropriate time to think about that, but yeah. Beau would've kept my ass in line like a drill sergeant. And I would've loved every second of it.

Lincoln white-knuckled the arms of the chair and then sprang to his feet as if he couldn't control himself. He paced in the area behind the chairs. "Why didn't you say something sooner?" The question was ripped from his throat in barely contained anger.

"I thought I could handle it." She bumped my shoulder. "Cal pointed out I should come to you. That the three of us are stronger together."

Teague's nostrils flared as he gripped his knees.

"We have to stop playing his game," she said. "Teague, you're the only one who really stands up to Father. Lincoln and I took the easier route just trying to make him happy. But we can't let him continue to control our lives."

"If I have to barricade the church doors—"

"She isn't marrying that son of a bitch." I spoke without thought despite the words were true. Even if we hadn't already taken vows, I wouldn't have ever let her anywhere near that bastard again.

"Glad we're in agreement there," Teague said.

"Lincoln," she said, softening her tone. "You should sit."

He paused pacing for a moment, but shook his head. Beau pushed off the desk and stood between her brothers, taking one of each of their hands in hers.

"Do you have the photos?" She looked at me.

I pulled out my phone and scrolled to the images of the damage he'd inflicted on her. I held up my phone, unable to look at the pictures for more than a second. My rage wouldn't help things now, but I really wanted to thrash this room to pieces.

"You said you hit your jaw on a desk." Lincoln spoke carefully, but his anger was palpable. Like he was barely containing it.

I moved on to the pictures of her arm and wrist before pocketing my phone. If I let them look much longer, they were going to explode. At least now I could see with my own eyes what I had thought.

If they'd known he'd hurt her, they would've unleashed holy hell on Alex Davenport.

"He touched you," Lincoln grated out, staring at her still-bruised face.

"Are you all right?" Teague asked through his teeth.

"I will be."

Her throat worked as she swallowed. "Father saw . . ." She hesitated as she tried to collect herself. "He saw Alex force himself on me. Saw him do that." She shuddered. "He didn't stop it. And he's still pressing for the wedding to move forward."

Teague bolted from his seat. "Son. Of. A. Bitch."

He picked up a paper weight and then seemed to realize it wasn't his to hurl. He slammed it back on the desk. "You aren't ever going to see either of them again."

Glad we were on the same page about that too.

She gripped Teague's arms. "I love you for being so mad on my behalf. But we have to think how we can use this to our advantage. How we can end this once and for all. Don't you want to be free?"

"Yeah. I do. But not if it means my sister gets used as a punching bag."

"You said he forced himself on you. Did he . . ." Lincoln trailed off as if the vile word was too much for him to speak.

"Just kissed. And touched," she croaked.

Kissing was sacred to her, and that bastard had stolen that from her. No man had the right to take what wasn't freely given. No man had the right to hurt innocent people.

I'd known we were going to discuss this, but reliving it was going to give me a heart attack. Or stroke. My heart raced as the fear she'd had that night pummeled my brain.

I needed to hold her. To feel that she was safe.

But her brothers needed that reassurance too.

Teague pointed at me. "You knew about this and didn't say anything?"

His wrath was easier to take because if I were in his shoes, I'd feel the same way. He had to direct all that anger somewhere, and I was the easiest target.

"I follow Beau's lead." I folded my arms over my chest.

"I knew how upset you'd be." She touched his shoulder. "Both of you are always trying to protect me. I just wanted to do the same for you."

"That was the wrong way to go about it." Lincoln pulled her into his arms. "No more secrets, please."

She squeezed him. "Same goes for you too."

He sighed but nodded. "I'm assuming you didn't go to the authorities about this."

"No."

"Do you have a plan?"

My respect for Lincoln ramped up a notch. He didn't try to run all over his sister—not that he could. I liked that he asked her thoughts, that he seemed to want to move forward as a team.

"My gut tells me we should all act normal until we figure out what to do," she said. "We need the element of surprise. Or any advantage we can get."

"I say we just end it now. You still have bruises on your face. We can prosecute the hell out of Davenport and disown that spawn of the devil we're lucky enough to have as a father." Teague moved to the windows and stared out at the park across the street.

"Kane Zegas will help us." Lincoln pulled out his phone.

Beau placed a hand on his arm. "You're going to think I'm crazy, but what about the company? The people who work there are innocent, and we've sacrificed everything to build it to where it is. What

Alex did won't hurt us, but if we go rogue on Father, Hollingsworth Properties could take a serious hit. We'll look unstable."

"If it keeps all of my family safe and gets rid of him in the process, I don't give a damn about the company."

My brows shot up at Lincoln's statement.

"Take a minute to think that through," Beau said quietly.

"I don't need it. Recently, I've been shown what's truly important. I love our work, love working with you, but I love our family more."

As I'd ridden up the elevator on what might as well have been another planet, I'd thought there was nothing I could have in common with these people. I should've known better, considering Teague was one of them and we'd always been friends.

But now, I realized we had a lot more in common than not. Our biggest differences were the size of our bank accounts . . . and that was irrelevant.

These three cared about each other the way I cared about my brothers and Ma. We all had moments of poor judgment in the name of protection, but it came from the right place.

"Pardon me for the interruption." Daniel's large form took up the entire doorway. "Your father is here, demanding to see you."

CHAPTER EIGHT

BEAU

"SEND HIM AWAY."

My tone sounded feral when I spoke.

"I'll let security downstairs know." Daniel turned on his heel.

"Wait," Teague said almost desperately. "Is he in the building?"

He twisted back around. "Just in the lobby."

"I'll be back." Teague hustled toward the door. "I have to go check on Pepper and Miss Adeline."

Panic swept through me. "You should call Lexie. Have them come here since Father can get in your building." I tried to put on a brave face. "Do you mind, Daniel?"

"Of course not. Let me know her location, and I'll have someone escort them."

Lincoln was already on the phone, murmuring.

And there was Cal. Still leaning against the desk. He hadn't intruded on our discussion. He'd simply been there for support.

Who was I gonna move on to? There is no one better than you.

I needed him. Needed the safety and comfort of his strong arms.

If I was going to get through the next few days, I had to have all the strength I could muster. And even if my emotional state was in tatters when it came to him, I had to take it moment by moment.

I shimmied between the two chairs.

His eyes flashed with heat as I moved to him with more confidence than I felt. I slid my arms around his waist and rested my head against his chest.

Those arms I wanted so desperately banded around me like a cocoon.

"You made the hard part look easy, baby sister." He spoke against my hair with a reverence that weakened my knees.

I didn't say anything, simply clung to him like he was the only thing anchoring me to sanity. He rubbed his big hands up and down my spine.

Like a support.

A partner.

A husband.

"You rescued Eric." Lincoln's stern voice was right behind us and I stiffened. "You've helped Beau in some capacity when she wouldn't come to us. But you clearly hurt her at some point."

I turned in Cal's arms and faced my brother. In typical Lincoln fashion, he was hard to read, but it was impossible to mistake how much he cared for me.

"All I've ever wanted is what's best for Beau."

There was no uncertainty in Cal's words. No apology or hesitation. I would have previously thought that that statement totally contradicted how he'd ended things all those years ago. But this was a lot easier to accept knowing what I did now. *He's shown you over and over since you've been back.*

"As long as you give that to her, we'll have no problems." Lincoln extended a hand to Cal.

I gaped.

This was the equivalent of a blessing. One I hadn't realized I'd want from my brothers because I never thought I'd be in a serious relationship again.

You're not in one now.

Maybe it was pretend, but it didn't feel that way.

Lincoln turned his gaze to me. "You don't have to hide what makes you happy." He reached for my hand. "You don't have to hide anything at all."

"We're married," I blurted.

Cal jolted behind me but kept a steady hold on my hip.

Lincoln's brows shot up.

"Just since this morning," I rambled. "I couldn't see any other way out of marrying Alex. And obviously, I can't marry him if I'm already married."

Understanding dawned in my brother's eyes, but as he scanned the way Cal held me, I wondered what he saw.

Did we look like we'd been forced into holy matrimony?

"He's threatened Cal's family too," I whispered.

Cal went rigid behind me.

Lincoln drew in a long breath. Looked at Cal with intent. He knew Father well, so he understood that Cal threatened something Father wanted to achieve. In this case, controlling me. And making money in another business venture. "Then I suppose Father has further threatened our family too, brother."

The last thing I'd expected was his easy acceptance of Cal. Maybe Lexie and Eric had had more of an effect on Lincoln than I'd realized.

"It's petty, but I want to humiliate Father and Alex by not showing up at the wedding," I said quietly.

That would send our father into a tirade. A well-deserved fit.

But nothing could repair all the damage he'd caused.

"And to do that, we need to act normal." Lincoln pressed his lips together. He glanced at Cal, then focused on me. "Do you trust him implicitly?" He flicked his chin at Cal.

As our entire history flitted through my mind. Yes, he once shattered my trust and everything we were. Every single other thing he'd done had spoken of protection, of putting me first, of lo—nope. Wasn't going there. Not now.

Everything in the past few weeks had built that trust brick by brick. Even when he wouldn't touch me as I craved because I was injured. He'd put my well-being above all else.

I'd have to be blind and a fool not to see that.

"Yes."

Cal's heartbeat thumped against my back. I was surprised by my answer too, but if we were going to make this mess work, we had to trust each other.

This isn't a happily ever after forever, Beau.

No, it was a *this man has done everything I've needed and more lately* and I wouldn't forget that.

"I agree that we can't let down our employees, but maybe we can figure out a way to force him into early retirement," Lincoln said.

"I've spent so much time with the man, trying to find anything. There's nothing." I threw my hands up helplessly.

"He knows who killed our mother." Lincoln spoke so quietly I almost didn't hear him. "But I'm not sure if he's responsible."

I was grateful Cal was behind me. I leaned against him for support. This was more than Lincoln had said about our mom in years. He avoided the subject no matter how I pressed.

And this nugget wasn't exactly what I'd been looking for. I was more curious about what she was like.

But I'd take anything I could get.

As I stared at Lincoln, I realized I was more shocked he'd actually told me than what he'd said. Our father was capable of anything. Even murder.

CHAPTER NINE

CAL

"CAL, you gotta get me out of here."

I huddled in the corner of Daniel's study with the phone pressed to my ear. Joe's desperate voice nearly tore me apart.

I'd been so focused on Beau, I'd neglected my brother. But if I were honest with myself, he'd needed the time in jail to sober up and hopefully get himself straight.

As pained as he sounded, this was more like the man I recognized. One who was responsible and did the right thing.

"I'll do what I can, but it may take me a little time."

I had no idea what I could do. There hadn't been a hearing yet. I wasn't sure they'd set bail. I hadn't even found a lawyer.

I yanked on my hair.

"Can you put up bail money?" He lowered his voice. "You know those fertility treatments wiped me out."

He'd refinanced their house three times. I'd made more payments on it than I cared to admit because I wanted my brother to have the family he wanted, money be damned.

My gut twisted. "Yeah. I've got you." Where the hell was I going to come up with the cash for bail?

"Thanks." He was quiet a minute. "I'm sorry. I . . . I screwed up."

"We'll figure it out. Just don't hurt Ma or yourself anymore."

"My time is up. Will you come see me?"

I glanced at Beau surrounded by her family. Except we were family now. And I had people that needed me too.

"Yeah. I'll come see you."

I hung up the phone and stared at the wood paneled walls a minute. I rubbed my face, the weight of all of it catching up.

I didn't know what time it was, but I had a twenty-four-hour shift starting tomorrow morning. There was so much to get done. And how was I going to watch Beau?

I couldn't leave her on her own in case her father came after her. What was I gonna do? Tether her to me?

Damn it.

"Everything okay?"

I couldn't get used to her kindness. I'd been the target of her anger for all these weeks. This was the tone reserved for others. And I wasn't fool enough to believe some vows had erased the past.

But I'd take it.

I'd take her happy, mad, whatever.

She had enough to shoulder. I didn't want to burden her any more than she already was. But I wasn't going to have a marriage—real or fake—based on secrecy.

"Joe, my brother, he's—" I scrubbed my face again. "He's, uh, he's in jail."

She thumped me in the chest. "Why didn't you tell me?"

"When exactly was I supposed to do that? We've kinda had a lot going on and you don't particularly like talking to me all that much."

She leaned against the mantel. "I'd rather talk about your problems than face mine."

That I understood. Maybe I'd been doing the same thing.

"His wife cheated on him—"

"Christina?" she asked incredulously.

I lifted a brow, surprised she remembered them from so long ago. Especially since they'd never met.

"Yeah. Knocked up by his best friend too."

Her lips parted. "They've been married forever."

"I know." I dumped my phone back in my pocket. "Joe's had a real tough time with it."

"Rightly so." She snorted, sounding pissed off on my brother's behalf.

"I'm pretty sure she burnt their house down, but they've pegged it on Joe." I tapped my pocket. "That was him. He asked me to come see him."

"What's his lawyer say?"

Guilt seeped into me. "I haven't found him one yet."

She whistled. "Lincoln, what's Zegas's number? I know you have it on speed dial."

"Have you come to your senses about prosecuting Davenport?" he asked, his arm wrapped tight around Lexie.

"We'll get to him, but right now Cal's brother is in trouble."

"Who?" Teague asked. "I heard some stuff about Joe but wasn't sure if it was true."

"What did you hear?" I frowned. Teague and I hadn't exactly been on speaking terms lately, but I expected him to set all that aside when it came to important things. There were a million rumors about Joe going around. I thought Teague wouldn't participate in gossip, especially about my family.

"That he beat the shit out of Stanis. And rightly so."

"Anything else I need to know about?" I had my hackles up. We'd been friends for a long time, but I was out of sorts. Everything was upside down.

"That's it." Teague folded his arms. "Now that we're all cozy, why don't you start telling me about you and my sister?"

"It's none of our business," Pepper said quietly, even as she laced her fingers though his.

"She's—"

"A grown woman who knows when she needs us," she finished for him.

He clamped his mouth shut.

"If you want an apology from me, you aren't gonna get it." I had nothing to be sorry for. Maybe we shouldn't have snuck around. And maybe I had broken some sort of bro code I didn't know about. But Pepper was right. Me and Beau . . . we were our own business.

"Considering you're really related now, you two had better patch things up."

Everyone but me looked incredulously at Lincoln.

"What?" he asked. "It's true."

"Where did you pick up that phrase? Patch things up?" Lexie asked.

I was lost. The guy seemed formal, but it was common enough language that most people probably knew it.

He shrugged. "Probably from one of you."

"What do you mean really related?" Teague narrowed his gaze at his brother.

"Shall I rip the Band-Aid off?" Lincoln asked, looking at Beau.

She straightened. "Cal and I got married this morning.

An collective gasp filled the room.

Teague bolted from where he leaned against a chair. Pepper tried to catch his arm but was too late.

"What did you say?" He stalked toward us.

I had the urge to put Beau behind me, though he'd never hurt her and she was more than capable of taking up for both of us.

She rolled her eyes. "You heard me." She put a hand on his chest. "Would you prefer I marry Alex?" she asked sweetly.

"No, but you shouldn't be with him either."

"He just saved my ass. How about a little gratitude?"

She took up for me.

Teague looked as startled as I felt.

"He's not good enough for you." He scowled. "Nobody is."

His words were like a punch to the stomach, confirmation of what I'd known all along. I wasn't good enough for her. Never had been.

Somewhere the hope I hadn't realized I'd been holding on to, the hope that maybe I was, burst into oblivion.

"I'm keeping her from marrying that woman beater," I said darkly. "That's it."

Beau flinched.

Teague seemed somewhat satisfied. "That better be it."

"Woman beater?" Lexie rushed over. "Did he hit you?" Her gaze roved over Beau, looking for any indication. The moment she saw the bruises along Beau's jaw, she stepped back, horror on her features.

"I'm okay." Beau pulled her friend in for a hug.

"You can talk to me," Lexie said in her ear. "I know things have been crazy for all of us, but don't forget you have people who love you." She let go and her gaze zeroed in on me. "I don't know what kind of relationship you two have, but whatever it is, you better respect Beau."

I shuddered a little. That woman was more frightening than the threat of a punch from Teague.

"I do."

Lincoln held up his phone. "I'll call Zegas. You can fill him in on the pertinent details."

I guessed the threats were over, much to my relief.

He dialed before I could protest. I'd heard of that Zegas guy. He was notorious for getting criminals off the hook. And he probably cost a fortune. How the hell was I going to find the coin for that as well? I could only hope for a deferred payment setup. And then I looked at Teague and bristled again at the anger in his eyes. *You'd once been like a brother to me.*

"I don't like that you were sneaking around behind my back with my sister," Teague said where only I could hear.

"You've made that clear."

"But you're separating when we're sure it's safe for her?"

My nostrils flared. "I'm doing what she tells me."

While I wanted her to be free to return to normal life as soon as possible, part of me wanted her to need to stay married to me for an extended period. Probably was best I didn't let Teague in on that.

"Keep your hands off her."

"Should've told that Davenport ass that," I returned coolly.

"If I'd known anything about him, I would have."

"I plan to pay him a visit as soon as we figure out what angle we're playing. I'll let you know when." I might've married Beau without his blessing, but I could let him and Lincoln come with me to teach that scum to never lay his hands on a woman again. If it were up to me, the bastard wouldn't have a choice because I'd like to break his fingers off one by one.

"I'll be there."

"If you wanna move past all the bullshit, I'm game." I shoved my hands in my pockets.

Lincoln extended the phone. "Here's Zegas."

CHAPTER TEN

BEAU

"SPEND-THE-NIGHT PARTY."

Vivian clapped her hands as we dug into sandwiches from a nearby deli.

"We've invaded your home long enough," Lincoln said.

Our entire family was in the Elliotts' apartment. Literally. Nine humans and I'd lost count of how many dogs. But it had been at our hosts' insistence.

Cal gently pulled me to the side. "These people are nice, but we can't stay the night here."

We? As in he and I? Or everyone?

It was weird thinking of us as a *we*, even though technically we had been for about six hours.

"You know why we need to," I said.

His jaw worked. "Yeah. Your dad is a psychopath stalker. But I gotta go to work early in the morning. And as nice as this place is, we aren't living our lives locked up in Tribeca." His expression turned worried. "I have to go see Joe and check on Ma."

"Did Zegas think he could help him?"

We hadn't had much of a chance to talk because of the chaos. Most of the time had been spent lining up security details and schedules. All of us had lives to live. None of us wanted them to be dictated by one man any longer.

But we'd yet to figure out how to get out from under him once and for all.

"I'm not sure. I felt a little like I'd been slapped after the conversation." He rubbed his cheek.

I hadn't had much experience with the lawyer, but from what I knew of him, that was an accurate assessment. He was a lot to take in, but a brilliant attorney.

Cal ripped off a bite of his sandwich and seemed to swallow it without chewing. Was that because of being a fireman? I imagined they had a lot of interrupted meals.

"I'm supposed to meet them at four at the jail," he said after taking a swig of water. He checked his watch. "Which means I have to get going soon."

"I'll come with you." The words were out before I could think them through. Cal had been there for me. Going with him to see his incarcerated brother was the least I could do.

He blinked at me. I supposed I hadn't been the most supportive person since I'd been back. Mostly, I'd taken.

"It's probably safer if you stay here," he said slowly.

"I thought we weren't staying locked up in Tribeca?" I smiled sweetly.

"Maybe I should learn to keep my mouth shut," he muttered under his breath.

"Or use it for other things." My face flamed. I was flirting. And not making a secret that I wanted him. Two absolute no-nos.

He leaned in close. "Like kissing you."

It wasn't a question or suggestion. My lips tingled, desperate to feel his mouth on mine. Did he still kiss the same? Would it be like it used to be? Judging by the flutter in my stomach, it would be more . . . everything.

"Not that," I whispered. I meant what I'd said. I only kissed people I loved. And my feelings toward Cal were a jumbled knot I hadn't even begun to untangle.

His lips ghosted my cheek. "Definitely that."

When he pulled back, I missed his heat. Felt the loss of his nearness.

And shuddered.

Because Garrett Calhoun didn't make empty promises.

"THERE'S someone you need to meet."

Cal turned off the ignition and pushed open his door.

I studied the street of houses. They were nice. Neat. Normal. Kids rode their bikes in the distance. A few people were gathered on front stoops, animatedly chatting.

It was hard to process. This was a row of inanimate objects, yet they felt alive.

When I went to the house I'd grown up in, I always felt cold and hollow.

Here, it was the opposite.

If Mom would have lived, would our house have been different? I had to think it would've been better . . . unless Father eventually killed her spirit the way he did everything else.

Cal opened my car door and offered me a hand. Electricity zapped when our skin touched. It always had, but I'd let my anger tamp down the sensation before. Now that I'd let go of some of it, his touch was more potent.

Or was it because we were married?

Meaningless vows wouldn't change things, would they?

No, but he'd taken me into his protection the minute he said "I do." And I'd felt the strength of that from that moment too.

Once I was out of the truck, Cal didn't let go of my hand as we moved up the front walk. My heart pounded. He didn't have to tell me where we were.

At least when I'd met his father, there had been the element of surprise. I hadn't had time to worry if he'd like me or if I'd make a good impression.

As short as the walk was from the car to the front door, it was more than enough time for me to second-guess everything.

Cal's mother was the most important person in his life. What if she hated me? What if she loved me? What if I said the wrong thing or insulted her or brought up something I shouldn't?

"She's gonna love you," he said as if reading my thoughts. "It's better if we don't tell her we're married yet. I don't want to end up buried in the backyard."

I snickered. A grown man afraid of his mother. It spoke volumes about him. Good things. Not the ugly ones.

"Are you sure it wouldn't be me?"

"Nah. She always wanted a girl. She'd keep you around." He rang the bell once before turning the knob on the front door. "Ma, you in the kitchen?"

My stomach pitched as we stepped inside.

There was the scent of something sweet—maybe apple pie—in the air. And the walls were littered with pictures of their family. School portraits. Vacations. Studio images of their entire family throughout the years.

Home.

This was what a home was supposed to be.

"Is this you?" I pointed at a kid who looked like he was in elementary school . . . and his two front teeth were missing.

Cal's cheeks turned pink. "I-uh-I thought I was Batman." He rubbed the back of his neck. "My brothers dared me to jump off the roof if I was. Mike promised he'd catch me. He missed." He grinned and pointed to his teeth. "They were ready to come out anyway. And they grew back."

How had his mother put up with so much mischief?

"That's one of my favorite pictures."

I jumped at the sound of the woman's voice.

She pinched Cal's cheek. "I wanted to kill all of them at the time. Imagine seeing your baby boy flying by the kitchen window."

"All in one piece, Ma." Cal pulled her in for a hug.

"I don't know how." She swatted him before hugging him back.

When she released him, her gaze wandered to me. "Have you finally brought home a nice girl for me to meet?"

The blush on Cal's cheeks deepened. He linked his fingers with mine once more. His mother discreetly lifted a brow.

"Yeah. This is Beau."

She stared at me with an unreadable expression. I couldn't breathe. There was none of the warmth toward me that she had for her son. Her eyes felt like an X-ray machine examining every facet of my being.

"It's lovely to meet you, Mrs. Calhoun," I said shakily. If we'd have had this introduction back in my twenties, I would've been less nervous.

Maybe Cal hadn't been joking about her burying him in the backyard.

I looked down at my clothes. Maybe *I* was going to kill him. I hadn't showered in almost a day and a half. And I was wearing worn jeans and a sweater. He should've warned me so I could've at least had on something proper. Or at least spritzed some perfume.

"I never thought this day would come." She yanked me away from Cal and threw her arms around me.

I stood there stiffly for a moment, but her warmth was impossible to ignore. I'd never had a hug like this. A motherly one.

Slowly, I lifted my arms and circled them around her back. I closed my eyes and let Cal's mom hold me. Even the scent of her was one of home. She wasn't cloaked in expensive perfume or clothing. She was cloaked in love. She was a mom who loved fiercely. My eyes stung as I clung to this woman I'd never met. But I felt her acceptance. Felt the love she had for her children.

Felt what I'd been missing all my life.

A mom.

I swallowed around the knot in my throat.

"I hope you're hungry," she said, taking my hand. She led me to the kitchen. "You're both too thin."

I glanced back at Cal, who shrugged. His posture was indifferent, but something flickered in his eyes.

"Sit. Sit." She patted a chair and gave me a little shove.

Cal pulled out the seat next to me. It creaked when he sat, but he dwarfed the thing. There were scratches and a small burn mark on the table. Was that glitter?

And there were placemats. Ones for the season that looked homemade . . . like they'd seen a thousand meals at this table.

The Calhouns probably needed the table for twenty that my father had, but this one . . . I'd have given anything to have dinner at this table every night.

"She's a little overwhelming," Cal whispered.

I shook my head. "Not at all."

She carried a platter that had enough food for an army.

Cal pushed from his seat. "Let me get that." He took it from her hands and set it on the table. Then he moved to the cabinets and pulled out three plates and glasses.

I couldn't stop watching as he grabbed paper napkins from a holder on the counter and utensils from a drawer.

It wasn't that Lincoln or Teague wouldn't set the table, but in the house we'd grown up in, that was a menial task for hired help. At least that was Father's view.

Was this how happy families functioned? Obviously all wasn't perfect, but there was some sort of magic in this house. Everything about it screamed close family and love.

I wanted it so bad I could taste it.

"Get her more ice than that, Cal." She untied her apron and hooked it on the peg just inside the opening that separated the kitchen from the living room. She poured tea in my glass without asking and then piled my plate with more food than I'd eaten in the past week.

Once everyone was served, she reached for my hand and Cal's, then nodded at him. They bowed their heads and he said a quick grace. I'd only been to church for weddings or when Father had deemed it advantageous, but I'd never eaten a meal that had been blessed.

Reluctantly, I released her hand. She patted my thigh, and I swallowed hard again. Cal did that a lot, and I wondered if he'd picked it up from her. It was different when he made the gesture. This one was filled with motherly love.

I was so wrong.

The realization crashed on me like the house had collapsed. We should've never kept our relationship a secret. Not from his family, at least. We'd missed this. And it wasn't just me, although selfishly I wished I'd had this feeling for all these years.

Could I have called her just to talk? Would she have taught me how to cook? Would she have made room for Lincoln and Teague at her table? Yes. One hundred percent. Yes.

But if I'd been accepted into their family all those years ago, how much more painful would the loss of Cal have been? Because it wouldn't have just been him. It would've been all of them.

"Do you not like lasagna?" Her brow furrowed as she looked at my untouched plate.

"Thank you for having me," I said quietly.

She squeezed my thigh again. "Sweetheart, you're welcome here anytime."

Cal nudged my foot under the table in silent support. Sitting across from me was the man I fell in love with. The man who'd stolen my heart and never given it back.

And I knew that the ugly version of him had been a lie.

Because I'd never seen that Cal again.

CHAPTER ELEVEN

CAL

"I CAN'T COOK LIKE THAT."

Beau worried her lip in her teeth as we walked from Ma's to the truck.

I laughed. "I'm pretty sure not too many people can." I unlocked the door and held it open. "Sometimes I wonder if she sees invisible people or something. Because she cooks enough for the entire neighborhood every time."

She patted her stomach. "It was so good, but I thought I was going to throw up when she piled a third helping on my plate."

I groaned. "Ugh. Me too."

"Cal!"

I wheeled around.

"You forgot your leftovers." Ma held up three foil pans. Three. Like she wouldn't feed us again for a month.

I jogged back up the walk and took the pans before kissing her cheek.

She patted mine. "I like her."

Something in me warmed. I already knew she would, but hearing the words . . . it felt . . . good.

"Bring her back soon."

"Since we have all these leftovers, we don't have a reason to for a while." I grinned.

"Garrett Calhoun..."

"Love you, Ma. I'll call you later."

She went on her tiptoes and waved. "Bye, sweetheart. You come see me anytime."

Beau waved back. "I will."

"Mind holding this?" I placed the pans in Beau's lap and closed the door.

There were two SUVs parked a few houses in front and behind. They were older models that fit in the neighborhood. Ones that wouldn't draw attention.

I had to give credit to Daniel Elliott. He was smart.

And I had peace of mind knowing someone was watching over Ma when I wasn't there.

Especially when the black sedan was parked across the street.

I hesitated before I cranked the engine.

The windows of the car were so dark, I couldn't see if her father was inside. I doubted he'd get his hands dirty, but who knew?

And I felt guilty leaving Ma, even though the security detail was made up of ex-military special ops guys who could dismantle me before I could blink.

"Call your brother." I inclined my head toward the sedan.

Beau stiffened. "Should we go back inside?"

I stared straight ahead, torn between options. When it came to my family's safety, I wanted to be the one to take care of them. But I was running on no sleep. I couldn't be in a million places at once. And I had to learn to trust other people to carry some of this load. Especially expertly trained people.

I *knew* that the security team could do a better job than me at protecting Ma, but still couldn't shake the ingrained feeling I should be the one watching over her.

What was I going to do? Skip work tomorrow?

I couldn't. I had to scrape up bail money for Joe.

And I wasn't going to live under some asshole's iron rule. He'd dictated my life with Beau for too long. If it weren't for him, she wouldn't be my wife now. But if it weren't for him, maybe I'd have never had to let her go in the first place.

"Cal?"

"I should call Aaron. See if he can come stay with her tonight. I'm pretty sure he's off tomorrow."

We both pulled out our phones. And even after Lincoln was aware their father was watching Ma's and Aaron had agreed to stay with her, I didn't feel better as we drove away.

"We should take all this food to Daniel's where it will be appreciated," Beau said.

I sighed. She was right.

I was used to constantly being around people, whether it was my family or at the firehouse, but I needed some quiet.

"Tomorrow." It would make more sense for me to go grab a bag so we could stay with Teague or the Elliotts in their secure building. Because in the morning, I was going to have to drop Beau by there anyway.

But I wanted my shitty apartment.

After we did drive-bys of all my brothers' houses.

I turned up the radio and held up my hand, palm up. I needed Beau's strength and energy, but I couldn't just take it. She had to meet me in the middle.

When her delicate hand closed around mine, something in my chest eased. I'd been wound up tight for . . . I couldn't remember how long. But it was taking its toll.

She cracked her window, letting in some fresh night air, and leaned her head back against the seat.

A few minutes later, we rolled by Bobby's. There was security somewhere. I'd been promised. But they were so discreet, I couldn't make them out.

However there was no missing the black sedan parked across the street from my oldest brother's house.

"Son of a . . ." What had I expected? That her father's threats were empty promises?

We cruised to Mike's.

Another sedan with blacked-out windows.

"I'm sorry," Beau said when we passed by Ben's.

I squeezed her fingers.

"I think I'm so used to being followed, it just doesn't register." She shook her head. "That's crazy."

"*He's* crazy," I corrected. "Why does he do this to you?"

"I-I don't know. But I'm such a fool. I thought I'd learned to zig and zag enough to shake him. But I'm wrong." She rolled her chain between her fingers.

"Nobody is going to follow my wife around," I growled.

My wife.

I was getting way too comfortable with that term.

"How are you going to stop him?" she asked incredulously.

I turned onto Aaron's street. "Haven't figured that out yet."

My brother had texted he was at Ma's already, but there was another black sedan parked near his place.

Joe's house—or what was left of it—was a couple blocks away. Might as well see what was happening over there.

"I talked to Zegas while you had a minute alone with Joe."

I cut my eyes to her.

"I'll pay his fees and post bail. It's the least I can do, considering what you've given up for me," she said.

"*No*."

"It's already done."

I stomped on the brake at a yellow light.

"Then undo it."

She wasn't paying my way. I didn't want her money.

"This is the gas station all over again," she muttered.

"What are you talking about?"

"I tried to give you twenty bucks for gas and you went all broody."

Because it wasn't her place to take care of me. I was the one responsible. My father had provided for our family. Ma had never had to work a day in her life. And I wasn't going to be any different.

Not that I'd stop Beau from working.

I wanted her to have and do everything she wanted. Hadn't I already proven that? But her money was off-limits. Period.

"And then you dove for the backseat when your brother pulled up." It was a low blow, but that had stung.

Me and my old truck and my five bucks for gas weren't good enough.

"I was wrong," she said quietly. "I realized that at your mom's tonight. We never should've hidden anything. I should've stood up to my father back then. My brothers too. Things would've turned out different."

The light turned green and I sped off.

"No. They wouldn't have."

I could've given her love and family, but she was destined for more than that. *There is nothing more important than that.* Not in my world.

And seeing how she'd been with Ma, how hungry she looked for that motherly attention, maybe I'd screwed up not giving that to her before. It could've strengthened her.

She twisted in her seat. "They would have."

She sounded so sure, but she was wrong.

"Oh yeah? Tell me how," I challenged. It was a dangerous path. One we had no business going down. The past was just what it was. There was no changing it. "Never mind. There's no point."

"Did you ever love me?"

I pulled over in front of the rubble of Joe's house.

"That's the wrong question, baby sister." I stared at the charred dreams of my brother. Mine had burned to the ground a long time ago.

For a moment, she unshuttered her eyes and let me see all the pain I'd caused.

It was too much. I'd never wanted to hurt her, but it was the only way she'd been able to fly.

I let go of her hand. It was too much to touch her. It hurt to see all we'd lost. But how did we lose something that was never really ours to begin with?

She fisted her chain and dropped her chin to her chest. "That's what I thought."

She had it all wrong.

"The right question is: did I ever stop?"

CHAPTER TWELVE
BEAU

DID I EVER STOP?

Did I ever stop?

The words had been on repeat in my head since he'd spoken them. Streetlights and buildings blurred past. I couldn't focus on anything but those four words.

They couldn't be true.

I might not know the exact second he had stopped loving me, but I was well aware of the second I'd found out.

And then I thought about all of his behavior again.

That was the only moment he'd ever hurt me.

Sure, we'd bickered, but it was never vicious. Not like that.

That question bolstered my earlier theory.

He'd lied to me all those years ago.

He hadn't used me or grown tired of me. Cal had pushed me away. On purpose. He'd destroyed my faith in him. On purpose.

But why?

Why push me away as if I didn't matter, if he'd loved me? Yes, he said it was so I could find the happiness he thought I'd wanted, but was there no other solution? No way for us to be together while I did that? Did he believe our worlds wouldn't have been able to co-exist?

Was that it? Maybe his intention had been altruistic, but I was angry. At my father. At Alex Davenport. At being controlled.

At . . . the man who'd kept his heart from me.

He parked the truck.

I remained frozen in my seat, even when he opened the car door.

I clutched my chain. He'd always opened the door. Gentlemen did that.

Like my brothers.

Not calloused men who used women and threw them away.

My heart hammered in my chest. His rejection had crippled me. I hadn't fought for him, slayed by his words. Instead, I'd run. I'd begged and pleaded to get out of this city, away from any reminders of Garrett Calhoun.

That had been a fool's mission.

An ocean and a different continent hadn't made me forget.

Neither had time.

He'd rooted so deeply in me there had never been room for anyone else.

And he'd robbed us both of so much.

"You're a thief." I jumped down from the truck and shoved past him.

He caught me by the waist and held me as he locked the Suburban. It didn't help that I was loaded down with leftovers.

"I've never stolen anything." He lifted two of the pans from the stack.

Did he think that could keep me from escaping?

"Oh no?" I kept up with his long strides, following him down the street toward his apartment building.

It was the wrong way. I should've dumped this lasagna on him and gone back to my brothers. But his mother had worked hard to make it. For an afternoon I'd had a glimpse of what it would have been like to have a mom. And I wouldn't disrespect her.

"No," he said, as he held open the door to the building.

I stomped up the few flights of stairs like I'd been there a million times.

He balanced the two pans with one hand and jammed the key into the lock of his front door.

Once inside, he took my pan and set them in the refrigerator.

I followed him to the kitchen. The space between the fridge and the counter was almost too small to fit both of us.

Another mistake getting so close to him.

He smelled like everything I longed for. And damn him, he still made me feel safe.

"You stole my virginity."

"You gave it to me."

I lifted my chin, and he stared down at me.

"You stole our time together."

He flinched. "Wasn't ours to begin with."

How could he say that? We'd had everything at the tip of our fingers. I'd found us an apartment—one that would've been completely wrong. It wasn't like his Ma's house. Or even like this.

Once we'd finished renovating it, it would've been a museum . . . just like the house I'd grown up in. Because that was all I'd ever known.

I pushed at his chest. "You stole my heart."

"Wrong again, baby sister." He cupped my cheek with more gentleness than a man of his size should be able to.

I fisted his shirt. "You stole my choice."

He turned away so quickly, it was as if I'd slapped him. "I wouldn't—"

"If you never stopped loving me like you claim, then you did. We were supposed to be partners. A team. We could've figured it all out together." I shook him. "You took that choice from both of us."

His expression was hard, unfeeling. And he was silent.

I shook harder, which didn't move him an inch. "Do you hear me?"

And still he said nothing in return. As I stared up at him, he was the most beautiful man I'd ever seen. He still stirred something in my soul in a way no one else ever had. He made me happy. He made me mad. He made me safe. He made me *feel*.

We stood in this tiny kitchen with the laminate peeling off the counters and the wood cabinets worn from more years of use than either of us had been alive.

Was this what he'd wanted? Did he think I wouldn't have lived here with him? That it wasn't good enough?

"If this is where you wanted to be, I wouldn't have cared." My fists ached from holding his shirt so tightly. "I'd have followed you to the ends of the Earth."

"I know that."

I waited for more. Waited for him to elaborate. To make his actions then and now make sense.

The wall I'd erected around me all those years ago had served me well. It had several layers. Some of the outer walls, I allowed people behind. A very few, like Lexie, made it much deeper. No one had ever broken through to the very center of me.

Except Garrett.

He bulldozed it down twice.

Once when we'd met.

And the second when he'd sent that first text after I came back to New York.

The crazy thing was that this time, I'd actually had my guard up. It was useless. A crumbled mess.

I was standing in the middle of a sea of rubble.

Just like before, I had no guarantee of what was next. I was exposed. Vulnerable.

I'm keeping her from marrying that woman beater.

That was what he'd said to Teague. And it *was* the reason we'd gotten married.

I had no right to be hurt by his explanation, especially when it was the truth. But it did.

Why am I even here?

I should've gone back to Teague and Pepper's. Did I think because Cal and I had gotten married that we had an obligation to fulfill our vows? That this was real and we were supposed to fight to make this work?

Judging by my verbal diarrhea, yes, I did think that.

Which was ridiculous.

I released him like he'd burned me.

Because he had.

Cal had the power to make me short-circuit, to lose my head. And I had to figure out a work-around. Because he was my husband for the interim, and I couldn't avoid him.

The problem was, maybe I didn't want to. Because of his words... which might possibly match his actions.

That's the wrong question, baby sister. The right question is: did I ever stop?

What did I do with that?

CHAPTER THIRTEEN

CAL

"WANT LASAGNA FOR BREAKFAST?"

I hadn't said a word to Beau since we'd stood in my kitchen last night and she'd flung arrows of truth at close range. What I'd come up with now was pathetic, but the best I could do.

She stretched and yawned, my T-shirt she wore swallowing her whole. "No. I'm still stuffed." She grimaced.

Last night, she'd made herself at home, rifling through my drawers until she found something that would do as pajamas. She'd used my toothbrush. And she'd crawled into my bed as if it were ours.

The smart thing to have done would've been to sleep on the couch.

But because I couldn't resist being close to her, in the name of protection of course, I'd slid in beside her and had the best sleep since the last time she'd been in my bed.

No nightmares.

And I'd woken up draped over her, clutching her to me like a kid with a teddy bear.

I threw off the covers, desperate to get out of the bed before I did something stupid. Like touch her.

"You wanna shower first?" I asked gruffly. My tone was too harsh, like she was an annoyance. An inconvenience.

I was annoyed. But not at her. At myself.

I could still feel the way she'd clung to my shirt despite not having one on. And I could still see that tortured look in her eyes. She'd opened herself up to me. Let me see how much pain I'd caused her.

And I couldn't stand it.

If I thought that bastard Davenport hurting her had made me insane with anger, it was a thousand times worse knowing I'd done it.

"Go ahead," she said without looking at me.

I stalked to the bathroom and turned on the shower. I shoved my flannel pajama pants off and stepped behind the curtain without waiting for the water to warm.

I hissed when the cold spray hit me but forced myself to duck my head under the water.

I was pissed off that I had to leave her today.

My family wasn't the only one who'd had those black sedans watching their houses. There'd been one outside my place last night too. I hadn't said anything about it to Beau, pretty sure she'd seen it too.

If I had to guess, it was still there.

Now that her brothers were aware of exactly what was going on, they'd watch out for her. Somehow that wasn't good enough for me, but it would have to do.

"You don't have to take me to Teague's. It's too far out of the way for you."

I jolted at the sound of her voice and stuck my head out from behind the curtain. "I'm taking you."

She had my toothbrush stuck in her mouth again. And now I had a view of her long legs.

I ducked back into the shower, trying to erase the image from my mind. But it was already ingrained there.

She could be wearing a gown and high heels and made up to the nines, but it wouldn't compare to what I'd just seen. Her . . . comfortable and at home . . . with me.

Would it have been like this? With us? For us?

"It's kind of nice not having any stuff," she said around the toothbrush. "I don't have to lug anything around."

This woman had been beaten, stalked, controlled, and manipulated, yet she was making the best of it. I sure as hell wouldn't have had that attitude.

She's stronger than you ever hope to be.

I scrubbed shampoo over my head with more force than necessary. Yesterday, I was some chump with a boatload of problems but a life that was okay. Today, I was the chump that had everything I'd ever wanted . . . except she'd been forced into cementing herself in my world.

So I couldn't enjoy one of the best mornings of my life.

"Shit, that's cold."

Warmth pressed against my back and my body came to life.

"How do you stand this?" She reached around me and turned the hot water knob higher.

I didn't have the heart to tell her it wouldn't do any good. It would be another five minutes before it got hot.

"Used to it," I grunted. The cold had helped tamp down my arousal, but one touch from her and the chilly water was no competition.

Who was I kidding? It was her, brushing her teeth, that did it.

She shimmied around me and squeaked when the spray ran down her face. "One-hundred-degree weather. The scorching hot desert. The Everglades."

She seemed to hold her breath as she rinsed her hair. All I could focus on was the way her tits perked up when she lifted her hands to her hair.

Get a grip, Cal.

Oh, I wanted to get a grip all right. On her hips as I took her right here in this shower. Kiss her. Touch her. Bring her to an orgasm that would stay with her all day long. I was already wound up, imagining her moans of ecstasy.

Apparently, my body was completely on board with that.

And then I caught sight of the purple hue on the underside of her arm. Anger doused my desire. I couldn't touch her. Not when she was still hurt.

I squirted shampoo in my palm and massaged it into her wet hair. Her eyes flew open, but she made no move to stop me.

I tried to be clinical, which was impossible when it came to Beau. Her hair was like silk, even though it was wet. She hummed as I worked my fingers over her scalp. Goose bumps raised on her skin.

Something about knowing I had that effect on her . . . it satisfied something deep within.

She turned, and I shampooed her long hair. I tried to stay focused on the dark locks, but the smooth line of her back that gave way to her ass was too much to ignore.

She was perfect. So damn perfect.

How had I ever been lucky enough to hold her? To know her?

I threaded my fingers around the back of her skull and massaged.

"I hope you want to do this every day," she moaned, then stiffened as if she realized the implications of her words.

They'd slipped out.

And while I wanted to cling to them, they hurt. Because one day, she wouldn't be mine.

She's not yours.

But it sure as hell felt like she was.

CHAPTER FOURTEEN

BEAU

"MIND IF I RIDE ALONG TODAY?"

I polished off the last sip of my smoothie and batted my lashes at Lexie.

She grinned. "You're not driving."

"We could use the extra hands. We have a lot of deliveries to make." Eric wandered into Teague's kitchen, followed by his dogs Muffy and Millie.

"Nice bow tie today," I said. "I love the yellow."

Lexie wore a bright silk jumpsuit to match. As always, she was impeccably put together with a sense of style and grace that appeared effortless.

Lincoln strode in also wearing a yellow tie. The dogs swirled around his feet as he moved toward Lexie with determination. It couldn't have been more than three minutes since he'd seen her, but he pulled her into his side and kissed the top of her head.

How could something so joyful cause a bolt of pain?

I was so happy for the family they'd formed. That they had each other and so much love it radiated from them.

But my chest hurt.

Because I'd almost had that. It had slipped through my fingers.

You're the worst, Beau. And selfish.

I was. These were the people I loved most. Their happiness came above all else. While it wasn't wrong of me to want even a fraction of what they had, it was rotten to be jealous.

"I recognize that dress." Lincoln narrowed his gaze on me.

Lexie slapped him in the stomach. "No good morning to your sister either?"

His eyes darkened as he tipped her chin up. "I'll give you a good morning."

She blushed.

I cleared my throat. "I had to borrow some clothes." But I'd drawn the line at underwear. I was going without until I washed what I had and could buy more. "But I don't match."

"Hang on a sec." Eric raced from the room.

"We'll collect your things during our lunch break," Lincoln said, with an undercurrent of viciousness. It wasn't directed at me. Of that I was certain.

I waved him off. "I'll just buy some new things."

"No. We aren't cowering from him. You don't wish to stay there, and he needs to understand that."

My brows shot up. Lincoln and I rarely pushed back against our father. We'd found it made life easier, although I wasn't so certain of that now.

"Have you spoken to him?"

"He hasn't called." Lincoln rubbed his jaw. "I'm tempted to go to the office to keep him occupied so he doesn't have time to focus on you. But I'm concerned for Lexie and Eric's safety." The war within him was obvious.

And I couldn't stand him being torn between me and Lexie.

"Help us make the deliveries. He's going to do what he's going to do whether you occupy him or not."

Eric rushed back into the kitchen. He opened his palm, revealing a sunflower pin. "Now, you'll match."

He affixed it to my dress and admired his work.

"Thanks, pal." I shucked his shoulder.

"I can sit in the back today so you'll be more comfortable," he offered.

I linked arms with him and Lexie. "Nope. Girls in the back. Boys up front."

She grinned. "I like this plan. We can snack on the donuts." Then she frowned. "Although, if I keep consuming them like they're air, I'm going to have to get some new clothes."

"You can borrow some of my overalls." Pepper tugged on the strap of her denim overalls as she came into the kitchen. "There's lots of room to grow in them."

"Like a baby?" Teague asked hopefully.

Pepper paled. "Um . . ." She looked at her feet.

I understood her hesitation. I never thought about children because it just hadn't seemed like they were in the plan for me. And I was happy without them.

Pepper was similar. She had Miss Adeline and all their fur babies.

But my brothers should be fathers. A whole brood of kids should feel their love and learn to be as kind and caring and protective as they are.

Cal should be a dad.

The thought twisted my stomach. Family was so important to him. He'd be amazingly patient and such a good example. It was a sin he didn't have as many sons as he had brothers. A daughter might make him crazy, but he'd be everything to her that my father hadn't been for me.

"I told you I'd clear my social schedule to help raise them." Miss Adeline nudged her. "Is there any coffee in this place? I have a whole herd of dogs to walk."

"We're going to help you," Pepper said, putting a hand on her hip.

She shrugged. "I figured I was on my own while you work out this baby situation."

"There is no baby situation," Pepper said almost helplessly.

"Lincoln's the oldest. He and Lexie should go first." I rinsed out my glass and put it in the dishwasher. "We should get going. We have deliveries to make."

"Let's blow this popsicle stand." Eric looped a leash around Muffy's neck. "And this week at art class I'll make a painting for the baby. When will she be here?"

Lexie and Pepper appeared ready to pass out, but I liked the idea of having nieces and nephews to spoil.

I slung an arm around Eric's shoulders. "I think you've got a while. Besides, we have to pick out a room for her."

"You don't know she's a her."

"Fine. *His* room." I smiled sweetly.

"Excuse me." Pepper rushed from the room.

My amusement faded. "I didn't mean to upset her."

"Kids are scary," Miss Adeline said. "That's one reason I never had any."

She cleared the air some, but I didn't want my future sister-in-law to be down.

"I shouldn't have pushed." Teague yanked on his hair and disappeared after her.

"Maybe we should go first," Lincoln said quietly.

I gripped the counter, stunned those words had come out of my brother's mouth. Lexie looked at him as if he were an anomaly.

And I felt like an intruder on a private moment.

"Eric, let's get these two loaded." I motioned toward the dogs.

"Okay. Don't forget the cooler," he called to Lincoln as we headed for the door.

"I won't."

Things were happening at warp speed. Not so long ago, it had been just Lincoln, Teague, and me. Our family had grown by leaps and bounds . . . and showed no signs of stopping. Now all of us were married—well, Teague would be soon enough—and life seemed upside down.

Or maybe it was finally right side up.

CHAPTER FIFTEEN
CAL

"ANY PROBLEMS?"

"What? I can't hear you over Bobby McGee."

There was a lot of background noise.

"Are you okay?" I shouted, then looked around the back of the station to see if anyone was listening.

"Why wouldn't I be?" she yelled back.

"Is that Cal?" I heard someone ask in the background.

Suddenly the noise was quieter.

"It is."

"Can I talk to him?"

I didn't recognize the voice. Where the hell was she?

"Hi, Cal. Thank you for saving me."

And then the pieces clicked into place. Eric.

"I just unlocked a door, man. You were the brave one."

I shuddered thinking about what the guy had been through, but was glad he was okay.

"Can you show us around the fire station sometime? Miss Adeline is always talking about how awesome it is."

Somehow, I smiled. "Yeah. You name the time and we'll do it."

"Cool. Can I bring my dogs?"

"The guys would like that. And if you want, I'll show you how to turn on the siren in the truck."

"Awesome."

Family.

Eric was literally my family. I guessed technically he was my brother-in-law.

"You'll get the special family tour," I promised.

"Sis, can we go to the fire station today? Cal's gonna give us the family tour," he said proudly.

If he wanted to do it today, we could. But if I showed him around on my day off, we could go to Ma's to eat after. She'd like to meet him. All of them.

I rubbed my forehead. How was I gonna tell her I'd gotten married without her?

"She said we can't today. We have too many deliveries."

I hated the disappointment in his voice.

"Let me check the schedule. I'll let you know my days off and you can decide what works."

"All right. I'm going to let you talk to Beau now. Bye."

"Why would you think something is wrong?" she demanded. "Did something happen?"

"No." I sighed and leaned against my truck. "I get off at seven in the morning. I'm going to check on Ma, then I'll report for hair washing duty."

A barely audible gasp escaped her. "Not necessary."

The feel of her hair between my fingers was as vivid as if we were still in the shower. And I needed to douse those thoughts since I was at work.

"Have you seen Copper and the puppies?" Puppies. That should keep my brain off Beau's body.

"This morning before we left," she said.

"Anybody following you?" Her stalker father really should tamp down my desire. Oddly, it made me want to hold her even more.

"Yeah, but we're all good."

Brrrrriiiinnnngggg.

"Alarm's going off. I gotta run." My feet were already headed back to the station.

"Be careful."

I didn't miss the note of worry in her voice. It made me feel better and worse. I hated for her to be concerned and loved it at the same time.

"I will."

"MA. YOU UP?"

It was a little after seven. She got up at four every morning. Of course she was up.

"Just in time for breakfast."

She was in front of the stove, like always. And I was grateful for her consistency.

I kissed her cheek. "Where's Aaron?"

"He left for his shift a bit ago."

At least he'd stayed with her again. The security detail and the black sedan were still stationed out front. Did these people sleep?

I leaned on the counter as she pulled an egg frittata out of the oven. "You talk to Joe?"

"Yesterday. He sounds like himself again." She set the pan on the stove. "It's like he was in a trance."

That was exactly what it was like. I wasn't sure he even realized he'd drunk himself stupid and drove. At least not when he did it.

"He wants me to go by the hospital and see the lady and her child." She sliced the frittata, and I held a plate for her to pile it on. "I talked to my car insurance company. They gave me a list of body shops where I could get an estimate."

"I'll take it."

She touched my shoulder. "I can do it."

"They might give you the runaround and try to take advantage—"

"Don't you dare say of an old woman." She shook her spatula at me.

I held up both hands. "Wouldn't dream of it."

I took our plates to the table and grabbed a couple of forks. She sat down, reached for my hand, and said grace. When she finished, she kept her fingers around mine.

"What's my baby boy doing here so early on his day off?" She squeezed. "I didn't think I would ever get to meet her."

It was terrifying how well Ma could read me. I was here because of Beau. She had me so mixed up, I didn't know what to do. My instincts were pulling me in one direction and my head in another.

I let out a long breath. "I didn't think you were either," I finally said.

"She's why you've never found anyone else."

I paused with my fork halfway to my mouth.

She smirked. "Your father couldn't keep anything from me. I kept waiting and waiting for you to bring her home, but you never did."

"And you never said anything?" I asked incredulously.

"Your father told me not to meddle." She shrugged. "You know how I am."

I didn't think she had it in her not to get involved. She'd never been shy about sharing her opinions or inserting herself in our lives.

"He liked her. Said you seemed real happy. Even held her hand." She patted my arm.

I chewed slowly and swallowed. "I was happy."

Had I ever admitted that? With Beau, I'd been ridiculously happy. She just . . . she was special. It was like I'd held on to a star for a brief moment in time.

"And now you've reconnected?"

I tapped my foot. That was one way to put it. "I—hell, I don't know, Ma."

She beamed. "I was pretty sure the other day, but now I'm confident."

"About what?" I shoved eggs into my mouth.

"She's the one." Then she laughed. "She has you mixed up and turned about and I'm thrilled for you."

"I can't keep her," I said quietly.

Her expression turned serious. "Then why are you messing around?"

"I can't stay away."

"You better figure out a way to hold on to her," she said.

It was impossible. I just couldn't help myself. Garrett Calhoun . . . unicorn and rainbow chaser.

"I'm not good enough for her."

Ma's chair scraped when she stood. She clasped my face in both of her hands. "Don't you ever speak about my son that way."

My eyes rounded.

"Get that shocked look off your face. You're a good boy. Protective. Loyal. And don't think I don't know about how you foot the bill for all your brothers." She shook my face. "Any woman would be lucky to have you." Her gaze narrowed. "And if she said otherwise, *she's* the one not good enough for you."

She kissed my forehead and returned to her seat.

"She's never said that."

She hadn't. And she'd never acted that way either. Teague, on the other hand, had made his opinion clear. But I didn't much care what he thought. Beau was the one who mattered.

"Good." Ma forked a bite of frittata. "You need to stop carrying everyone's problems on your shoulders. They're grown men. It's time they figure out how to fix their messes themselves so you can focus on your own happiness."

"I'm not happy unless my family is."

Her eyes got glassy. "Your father is so proud of you."

I glanced away and swallowed around the lump in my throat. "I let him down. I couldn't save him."

"Oh, Cal. It was an accident. A terrible, cruel accident. You did all you could. No one blames you."

Her words were meant to soothe, but I couldn't believe her. It was my fault. And if they didn't blame me, they should.

"It should've been me. You and Pop had plans. He was gonna take you on a cruise." My fork clattered to the table. I couldn't eat anymore.

"He'd be devastated to hear you say that. If anything, he wanted you to have the best life in the world. And he'd be furious to hear you gave up on that girl because you don't think you're good enough." She pushed her plate away. "And we shouldn't have planned to take that damn cruise. We should've done it. Life is too short."

Every sentence was like a slap in the face. Pop's death had made me realize just how precious life was. But it hadn't mattered because I'd lost the person I lived for. I trudged on because I loved my family and my job.

What good was any of it without Beau?

"Ma?"

"What is it, baby boy?"

I wasn't good enough for Beau, but I wasn't going to let any more life pass me by.

"I need Grandma Calhoun's ring."

CHAPTER SIXTEEN

BEAU

"WOULD YOU RATHER STAY HERE?"

I lifted a brow at Cal's question. Teague's apartment was chaos. There were people and dogs everywhere. And it wasn't a small space.

I *did* want to stay.

But I also wanted to go back to Cal's. His place was like a cocoon. It had come to represent safety. I liked being in his space because it gave me a glimpse of him. The inner sanctum, everyday him. I understood him in some way when I was at his apartment and I hadn't even snooped yet.

"I would."

He nodded without argument.

Lincoln approached with Muffy on his heels. "Are you ready to go?"

"Yes."

It was Cal's turn to look confused. "I thought we were staying here."

"We are." I flicked my chin toward my brother. "Lincoln is going with me to get my things."

"No."

The simple word held so much power, it rattled me.

I nudged Lincoln. "Guess we should've made that lunch pit stop after all." He and I had decided it was best not to have Lexie or Eric anywhere near our father's home. We didn't want him to shatter any of Eric's innocence or try to taint Lexie in any way.

Cal seemed to get taller and bigger. "You were going without telling me?"

"I'm pleased to see you take your role as husband quite seriously."

I looked at Lincoln incredulously. He stared back.

"I thought you said it was kind of nice not having any stuff?" Cal challenged.

"It's become a matter of principle." I shrugged and looked down at my dress. "As much as I love Lexie's clothes, it occurred to me earlier that you've probably ripped all of them off her, and no offense"—I smiled sweetly at my brother—"it gives me a little bit of an icky feeling." I shuddered.

A secretive curve shaped his lips. "That was probably a good revelation."

"I'll drive," Cal said.

"You aren't going," I fired back.

"The hell I'm not. Did you not hear me when I said you weren't going anywhere near that son of a bitch again?"

The entire room fell silent. Even the dogs stilled for a moment.

"There's just something about firemen," Miss Adeline said with an appreciative glance in Cal's direction. Pepper elbowed her.

"Oh, I heard you," I said, my temper rising. "Just because we're married on paper doesn't mean you get to tell me what to do."

Cal inhaled deeply and sucked in his cheeks like he was praying for calm and the strength to hold his tongue.

His gaze seared me. "It doesn't matter if we're married with lollipop rings or rings dripping with diamonds, I made vows and I'm keeping them."

My breath hitched. That could've been the nicest thing anyone had ever said to me.

"Honey, if you can resist that, you're the strongest woman in the world." Miss Adeline fanned herself.

Well, I wasn't.

"Let's go." I glided to the front door with purposeful strides.

"Where are you going?" Teague asked.

"To get my things," I said over my shoulder.

"Not without me." He kissed Pepper and was right behind me.

The elevator ride to the garage was silent. There was a piece of me that didn't want to go. I *could* buy new things. But a bigger piece was tired of hiding.

Cal reached for my hand when the elevator doors opened. I wasn't sure if he sensed I needed his touch or if he needed mine.

I practically had to run to keep up as he stalked toward his truck. He held open my door and secured me in before clearing out some space in the back seat.

He fired up the engine, and I turned down the radio before one of our old songs could play. That was Cal's and mine; I wasn't ready to share that with anyone, not even my brothers.

"What's the plan here?" Cal asked as he drove up the ramp.

"Good question," Teague said. A tinge of annoyance at being left out was evident in his voice.

"We escort Beau to collect her belongings and we leave," Lincoln said with more confidence than I had.

"You really think it's going down that way?" Teague asked incredulously.

"You wanted the plan. I don't know how reality will turn out."

A pit formed in my stomach. I didn't want to see my father. We should've called Winston to find out when Father wasn't home. But avoidance and fear was how I'd gotten here in the first place.

I twisted in my seat. "Do you know why he wants the Davenports' company?"

"Does anyone know why he does anything?" Teague threw his hands up.

"They have an excellent reputation as contractors. That fits with the development aspect of Hollingsworth Properties," Lincoln said.

"I still haven't figured out how I was supposed to steal their company." It was baffling. If Father wanted it so badly, why didn't he do it himself?

Because he can't put himself at risk.

But his daughter was disposable.

"Don't bother trying to get into his warped mind." Teague gripped his thighs.

"I know you hate this house." Awkwardly, I patted his knee. "Thank you for doing this. All of you."

"You don't ever have to thank me for doing my job as your brother." He covered my hand and gently squeezed. "I'm pissed you're married to him." He inclined his head toward Cal. "But I love you too much to let that get in the way."

Teague had such a kind heart. Lincoln too. Maybe it was the way we'd grown up, but we knew the importance of our relationship. None of us took it for granted.

"Love you too. Both of you. Even if you are giant pains in my rear."

"I recall you didn't speak to me after I said that about you." There was a smile in Lincoln's voice.

"You said I was annoying. That's different," I huffed, but I felt lighter.

"Naturally," Lincoln said.

Cal had been quiet, focused on the street ahead. I appreciated his instinct that I needed a minute with my brothers. That he respected that.

He turned onto Father's street. The house loomed ahead, and I second-guessed if this was the right move.

I'd never arrived unannounced.

I'd never disobeyed his wishes.

I'd never shown up with the equivalent of a security team comprised of my brothers and Cal.

I'd never fought him this hard.

So much for acting normal.

Cal parked the truck in front of the house. I hated it. Hated that I had so few good memories. What would I have done without Lincoln and Teague? At least they had some recollection of Mom. I wasn't even fortunate enough to have that.

"I want him to think I'm marrying Alex."

I felt three pairs of eyes on me.

"Why?" Teague asked. There was no anger in his tone. He simply wanted to understand.

An idea had been forming in my mind. Before, it had been about humiliating the Davenports and my father. But this was an opportunity for something more.

"I . . . I want to do something. I haven't quite worked it out yet, but it's important."

"Your show." Cal's voice was strained, but I appreciated that he supported my wishes.

He pushed open his door and came around to open mine.

I led the way up the front walk with the three of them behind me. My legs trembled with every step, but I drew strength from the men who were there for me no matter what.

I tried to turn the doorknob, just like Cal had at his mom's house, but it was locked.

The muted chimes seeped through the thick front door when I rang the bell.

What felt like an eternity later, Winston appeared.

"The chicks have come home." He glanced over my shoulder. "And brought friends, I see."

I kissed his cheek when he stepped aside. "Hello, Winston." What would this house of horrors have been like without him?

"He awaits you in the drawing room." He gestured in the direction.

He can keep waiting.

"I just came to get my things. He promised I could stay with Teague before the wedding." I sounded like a teenage girl instead of a grown woman. But it was the way I'd behaved when it came to my father. Like he had the final say over my life. Because I'd let him.

I could pretend a few more days.

Now I was doing it on my terms.

I hurried up the stairs, my heels clicking on the hardwood floor.

The heavy footsteps of Cal, Lincoln, and Teague were right behind me.

Winston didn't argue.

The portraits lining the upstairs hallway had always creeped me out. Sometimes I swore my ancestors were watching me, even though I knew it was impossible.

I'd chased Teague and Lincoln up and down this hall when we were little and *he* was away. They'd helped me with my homework and played tea party. And as we'd gotten older, we'd hung out in the backyard and talked. It was here we'd become more than brothers and sister. We'd become friends.

If *he* hadn't been the way he was, would I have the relationship with my brothers I did today?

I touched an antique chest. Would this be the last time I set foot in this house?

I'd almost made it to my room, when Father appeared like he'd stepped out of the walls. Had Winston lied about him being in the drawing room?

"My errant, errant daughter. What have you done?"

CHAPTER SEVENTEEN
CAL

I BALLED my fists at my sides.

No one spoke to Beau that way. Especially not him.

I stepped closer to her, wanting her to feel I was near, at the ready for whatever she needed.

He flicked his gaze at me and scowled as if I were a piece of trash. And I wasn't too big to admit that look was powerful. It made me feel like I was nothing. Nobody.

But my pride didn't matter. Not when it came to her.

And he was garbage for forcing his hand.

"How brazen of you to bring your riffraff lover into my home."

"I asked him to come," Teague said, standing shoulder to shoulder with me.

Teague wasn't a lying type of guy, but if he felt it was necessary, I'd play along.

Beau touched her father's arm and had the most serene look on her face. Like she didn't mind being in this house or his presence. If I didn't know better, I'd almost think they had a good relationship.

"Daddy, I needed a few days to come to terms with the wedding."

Please let that be a lie.

Because if it wasn't, I was going to kill someone.

He looked at her as if he wasn't buying it.

She tipped her head down, a submissive move, before lifting her gaze to him. "I know I've resisted. It's all so sudden, and I haven't been in a relationship because I'm afraid of losing someone the way you lost Mother."

Whoa.

If there wasn't some truth in her words, she was a skilled actress. Even I believed her. Except she'd never once held back with me. Never showed an ounce of fear when it came to expressing how she felt. Even the past few days she'd been nothing but honestly raw.

You stole my heart.

It still shocked me she'd ever seen anything in me worth loving.

And I wasn't the only one affected by her. Something flickered in Samuel Hollingsworth's eyes. It was a flash of emotion I wouldn't have thought him capable of.

"I wouldn't ever wish that upon you."

Then why the hell would you watch while that bastard touched her?

"You always want what's best for me. I'm just stubborn."

He closed his eyes as if in pain. "So much like your mother."

I was caught completely off guard. I'd been ready for a showdown, or at the very least, some unpleasant words. The man was good at manipulation. I'd give him that.

There was zero room to doubt he loved his dead wife. I could see it.

His daughter? Whatever he felt for her was warped and twisted. Maybe he thought it was love, but I didn't.

"I'm sorry." She took his hands. "But I used these few days to get myself sorted."

Lincoln looked like a stone and Teague as if he was a ball of barely contained fury.

"Thank you for making this so easy. I've been ungrateful, and I see that now."

I'd never ever seen this side of Beau. She was soft and demure. And I hoped like hell she was full of shit.

I loved her fire. Even at her most vulnerable, she sparked.

This was as if some other woman had invaded her body.

"I'm pleased to hear that, though time will tell."

Her laughter tinkled in the hallway. "Don't be silly, Daddy."

"This is not a joking matter."

She kissed his cheek. "Loosen up. Like when we went dress shopping. That was fun."

The lines around the man's eyes relaxed. "It was nice."

"You promised I could stay with Teague. And since Alex and I will live here after the wedding, I'd like to do it now, please."

No. No. No.

Beau should never have to act this way with anyone. Never have to ask permission to live her life. She was too bold. Too wild and free.

I opened my mouth to say as much, but she'd asked us to play along. I'd told her it was her show, and I meant it, even if I didn't much care for this.

"I've had a long talk with Teague and Lincoln. They understand this is what I want and fully support my decision." She lifted their joined hands. "I hope being back in New York, we can focus on our family again." She glanced back at Teague with some sort of unspoken message.

"How does he factor into the equation?" Her father's nostrils flared when he flicked his chin at me.

"He's a friend of Teague's who was kind enough to offer to help me get a few of my things." She gave me a sweet smile.

I swallowed down the growl that rippled up my throat.

And all those things I was getting were going straight to our place. Where they belonged.

I froze.

The thought had come without hesitation. My apartment was a dump, but Beau had never once complained. She did belong there. She'd made herself at home. In a few days, she'd made the place a home.

"You won't interfere in her future."

Or I will screw your world up so fast you won't see it coming.

That was what he didn't say. But I had little doubt he'd make good on the undercurrent of his threat.

"Never."

And that was a promise I could keep. Because I would never do anything to keep Beau from having everything she wanted and then some.

"Very well." He focused on his daughter again. "I have some things your mother wanted to be yours. They're in my study."

There was a slight hitch to the rise and fall of her chest. And though I couldn't see but one side of her face, I recognized the hunger.

This man was a cruel bastard.

He knew her weakness. Knew she was starved for anything having to do with her mother.

"I'll get them after we collect my things," she said almost breathlessly.

"I have some items for the two of you as well."

The woman had been gone for a very long time. Why was he just now giving their children pieces of what was hers?

Even Teague's angry stance relaxed the slightest fraction. I got it. If Ma said she had something of Pop's to give me, I'd knock down walls to get to whatever it was.

I'd always thought nothing could take away the memories. But I'd been wrong.

Time could.

I couldn't remember some of the little everyday things about Pop, no matter how I tried. And I was desperate to hold on to everything. Every meal. Every moment spent together at the station. Each time he'd carved out to spend just with me.

But time was the ultimate thief.

I imagined it was that much worse for Teague and Lincoln. They'd been young when their mom died and didn't have as many memories. If they lost those, it was like she'd be permanently gone.

"Come to my study." He softened his features. "My dear, join us when you've finished packing."

And what was I supposed to do? I hated I'd looked for any direction from this man, but I better understood the dynamic after spending such a short while with them.

It was almost like the man held some sort of power. I hadn't figured out why all of them didn't tell him to take a hike, but now it made more sense.

And no one ever truly wanted to sever a relationship with their only remaining parent. I'd guess that was worse when a person had already lost one.

Family was everything.

Thick and thin. Better or worse.

And Beau was part of mine now. I wouldn't let her father use his mind tricks or manipulation on me.

Teague and Lincoln followed their father down the hall. I took a few steps behind Beau toward what I assumed was her bedroom. Discreetly, she shook her head.

We're playing it normal. Whatever that was.

I made a face of displeasure, making my feelings clear, before I moved to the wall on the opposite side of the hall. I leaned against it between two portraits with my arms folded.

And then her door slammed.

CHAPTER EIGHTEEN

BEAU

A HAND COVERED MY MOUTH.

My scream was nothing more than a puff of air, absorbed by that hand and the thick walls of the bedroom. Pain raced up my jaw from the pressure.

He spun me, forcing my front into the door, and caging me against it.

"I've missed you, sweetheart."

Alex's breath hit my ear as his lips moved against the rim.

How?

How had Father known I was coming? When I was coming? He'd set this up. Allowed this maniac in my space.

And I'd turned Cal away for the sake of looking normal.

I'd been stupid to ever think I could be even a single step ahead of my father.

"Part of me hopes you meant that little speech out there. It was lovely to hear you're so eager to be my wife." He sank his teeth into my earlobe. "But part of me is looking forward to how much fun it's going to be to tame you."

That crippling fear I'd felt before slammed into me with a

vengeance. All the places he'd hurt me throbbed in pain. They were not-so-subtle reminders of what he was capable of.

I wriggled, trying to break free.

"Fight me," he whispered darkly.

I tried to scream again, but it was a waste of effort. My heart pounded so hard it hurt.

Trapped.

He was too strong. Had me pinned with his body, as if he knew how to expertly use it to subdue.

No.

The sickly feeling intensified. Had he done this to other women? Made them feel helpless? Taken them against their will? Hurt them?

And what could he do to me in minutes?

Nothing.

I was going to try my best not to let him do this again. Anger, red hot and potent, submerged my fear.

I rocked back, trying to create some space between me and the wall.

Break free. Break free.

"That's it." His voice was a sick whisper. "In a few short days, we'll get to do this as often as I like."

He pressed me farther into the wall. Bile rose up my throat at the feel of his erection against my ass.

I could barely breathe. His hand still covered my mouth. I'd turned my head and one cheek was shoved against the wall.

Fight, Beau. Fight.

Humiliation washed over me at my helplessness.

You're the bravest, strongest person I've ever met.

Garrett's words came back to me, renewing my resolve. He believed in me. I believed in me.

Garrett.

I banged on the door with both fists.

I got in a couple of good whacks before Alex secured my wrists with his hands.

"Don't be stupid," he hissed.

With all my strength, I stomped on his foot with the spiked heel of my shoe. He howled in pain and slammed my head against the door. Stars dotted my vision.

The doorknob rattled, the massive wood flinging back.

Alex and I tumbled to the ground with the force.

Garrett.

He loomed over us. His face was red and his breaths were harsh when his eyes met mine.

"It's time you play with somebody your own size."

He grabbed Alex by the front of his shirt and lifted him as if he weighed nothing. Alex squirmed, landing hits and kicks to Cal's arms and legs that he didn't seem to feel.

Cal smashed Alex into the wall so hard it dented the plaster.

Alex screamed the way I'd wanted to.

"You think that's gonna help?" Cal growled. He gripped Alex by the jaw and squeezed. "How do you like that? Hurts, don't it?"

The crack of bones reverberated through the room. My stomach pitched, but it had nothing to do with Alex and everything to do with worry for Cal.

All the fight immediately went out of Alex. He closed his eyes, and for a second, I thought he'd passed out.

Then Cal snapped both his arms like they were twigs.

"What did he do this time?" Cal asked gruffly.

"Slammed my head against the door," I said quietly.

Teague and Lincoln burst into my room.

"You." Teague pointed at Davenport with a feral look in his eyes. He looked between me and Cal.

Alex whimpered.

Lincoln was focused solely on me. I'd seen him angry, but not this . . . I couldn't describe it. Murderous. That was what was in the rigid set of his jaw. "I'd like to know why he thinks he can touch you."

"You are going to regret the day you ever laid a finger on our sister, you sorry sack of shit," Teague said through his teeth.

Lincoln's fist flew first. When it connected with Alex's jaw, his head ricocheted. He looked at Lincoln in dazed shock.

I'd never seen my oldest brother violent. Ever.

"My turn." Teague landed a vicious blow to Alex's gut.

Alex couldn't double over because Cal still held him like a rag doll.

The punches didn't seem to satisfy my brothers. If anything, their anger ramped up.

"Move," Cal said.

They stepped out of the way, and he rammed Alex's head into the door so hard it knocked him out.

Cal's eyes were wild and ferocious when they met mine. "Any justice you want to serve?"

My pounding heart nearly burst. He'd defended me. Fought for me. And was giving me a chance to fight for me too. Like a partner.

A husband.

It seemed cruel and violent to hit a man who was in Alex's condition, but the memory of his sick pleasure spurred me off the floor.

Cal slid to the side, still holding Alex in place. I reared my leg back as far as I could and kneed him in the crotch with all the strength I possessed.

Cal lifted a brow, silently asking if I was done.

I nodded.

He dropped Alex on the floor.

I collapsed into his arms.

Safe.

With Cal I was safe.

"I'm sorry, baby sister," he murmured against the top of my head. "I'm so damn sorry."

There was so much pain in his voice, I felt it to my core.

"What the hell happened?" Teague stood over Alex's crumpled form as if ready to subdue him when he woke up.

I pressed my head into Cal's chest in an attempt to dull the throbbing. "He was in here when I came to pack. He covered my mouth. I-I tried to scream." All the adrenaline flowed out of me in a torrent. It was replaced by the overwhelming fear.

"You've brought a violent ogre into my home."

I stiffened when Father appeared.

"I've phoned the authorities. You'll be prosecuted to the fullest extent." He narrowed his gaze on Cal, but I didn't miss the gleam of triumph there. *He set this up?*

"You have got to be kidding me. Davenport attacked Beau. He was in her room," Teague yelled.

Lincoln was wound so tight, he looked ready to attack. "You allowed this piece of scum into your daughter's bedroom—"

"And that man attacked him," my father growled, focusing again on Cal.

I held to him tighter. "If you do that, I'm prepared to press charges against him." I flicked my eyes to Alex, hardly able to think his name, let alone speak it.

Father scowled. "We won't sully our name with such minor indiscretions."

The pain in my chest was worse than anything Alex had done to me physically. How did this man still have the ability to hurt me? Why did I give him the power?

I'd had my head slammed against a door in his home. And if Cal hadn't been here . . . I couldn't even think about how far it could've gone.

"You're my father," I whispered, though it was useless. I'd said that to him before and it hadn't mattered.

Lincoln stepped into his face. "You will sign over Beau's quarter of Hollingsworth Properties immediately. And while you're at it, Teague's too."

Father snorted. "Why on earth would I do that?"

My brother looked as frightening as I'd ever seen him. "Because if you don't, the entire world will know that you allowed your daughter to be beaten in your own home. And that you're connected to your wife's murder."

CHAPTER NINETEEN
CAL

I HELD the ice pack against her head.

Damn it.

I'd known better than to play by her father's rules and ignore my instinct. Because of that, Beau had a bashed-in head.

We'd left that house hours ago, but I was still too wired to settle down. Still vibrating with rage like I'd never known.

I should've killed him.

And I should be concerned that the thought didn't bother me. I wanted him dead.

A broken jaw and arms wasn't justice for what he'd done to her.

Calm down. For her.

Teague had insisted we stay with them. I'd been too blinded with anger to argue.

Next on my hit list is that bastard Samuel Hollingsworth.

I'd stood there like a chump while he'd acted like Beau was at fault.

I will kill him.

That thought should've scared me too. But I'd spend the rest of my life behind bars if it freed her from that monster.

Judging by the rage radiating off Lincoln and Teague earlier, I'd have accomplices.

I stroked her soft hair, and she snuggled closer to me.

He'd set the whole damn thing up.

He'd known we were coming. All of us.

And he'd unleashed that son of a bitch on her.

How?

How could a father do that to his daughter?

How could he let a man he expected her to marry beat her?

How could he still be willing to hand her to him with his blessing?

Mine.

"I need you to promise me something," I said through my teeth. "And it's a big one."

She shifted so she could look at me. The ice pack fell to my chest. "What is it?"

"Never see him again. I know he's your father. I know you work for him, but I'm begging you. Please don't have anything to do with him." I sounded desperate. I *was* desperate. But I'd never rest if there was a possibility she'd be near him again.

I'd failed her. I wasn't sure I had the right to ask anything of her, but this, I would get on my knees and plead.

He'd put that hollowness in her eyes.

She'd barely said a word since we'd left that house, only speaking when spoken to.

It wasn't just the physical terror she'd been put through.

In some ways, her relationship with her father was like that of one with a sick parent. She'd been holding on to hope, praying he'd survive and he'd become the father she wanted.

But I hoped that this pulled the plug.

That whatever relationship they had was off life support.

It wasn't fair to ask her to willingly give up the only parent she'd ever known, but I had to.

"I promise."

The vow was spoken softly, but she was certain.

"I'm sorry."

"I should've cut him out of my life a long time ago." There was a sadness about her I wanted to take away.

"I meant for not protecting you. I promised you I would." I squeezed my eyes shut. "I let you down."

She was mine to keep safe.

I hadn't meant to, but I'd broken the vows I'd made to her before God. And because of that, there was a massive bruise forming on her forehead. I might as well have done it myself.

"It's not your fault."

"The hell it isn't," I roared before taking a deep breath to gain some composure. "I let you walk into that trap and didn't do a damn thing to stop you." I'd driven her there. Didn't that make me an accomplice?

The image of them on the floor. The fear on her face. The way her dress had been tangled up above her knees.

I couldn't get air. My chest felt like it was caving in on itself.

She was my responsibility.

And I didn't have the excuse of being blindsided.

I knew Alex was a threat.

I let everything else get in the way of taking care of it. If I hadn't, he'd have never been in the shape to find her, let alone touch her again.

What if he'd raped her?

I bolted from the bed, pretty sure I was going to throw up.

I made it to the bathroom and braced my hands on both sides of the sink. The man in the mirror was a stranger.

Something in me had changed the second I burst into her bedroom.

I was an animal. Wild and feral.

Consumed with the desire for revenge.

I wouldn't settle down until he was gone.

The savage in me had broken free and had an unsatiated need to rip two men to pieces.

And I wanted to hold Beau to shield her from any other threat.

But was I the real threat? I'd let her down.

I splashed water on my face, willing the nausea to go away.

"Garrett."

She touched my arm. It soothed and ignited that savage.

"I don't deserve to have you call me that."

Her haunted eyes met mine in the mirror. She shimmied between me and the sink. So fearless and bold. I'd never be half the person she was.

"You do." She slipped her arms around my waist.

I was supposed to be comforting her, yet here she was doing that for me.

The bruise on her forehead was more prominent under the bathroom lights. I held the sides of the porcelain pedestal sink so tightly I thought it might shatter.

"What you did..."

I hadn't wanted her to see that violence. I'd planned on paying the jackass a visit so she would be able to trust my word she wouldn't have to worry about him again.

"No one has ever supported me the way you do."

I looked away.

Her words were too painful, and I was barely hanging on as it was.

"I'll never forgive myself for letting him get his hands on you again." And I'd regret that until the day I died. Probably even past that.

She turned my face, forcing me to meet her gaze. "Stop that."

"How can you stand the sight of me?"

She pressed up on her toes and kissed my cheek. It burned my skin. She hadn't kissed me in any capacity in over a decade. I'd dreamed about that moment every night since I'd pushed her away. But now it hurt. Because I hadn't earned it. I wasn't what was best.

"You are so bullheaded."

How could she even have that ghost of a smile on her face at a time like this?

He could've fractured her skull. He could've—I swallowed down the bile. What if he'd killed her?

"Don't take up for me. Not now."

I needed her out of my space. Her sweet scent was choking me, a reminder of what I'd never have.

And what I needed so damn much.

I'd pushed her away once and it had taken everything I had. I didn't have it in me to do it again.

"I'll do whatever I want." She lifted her chin.

And it was another stab to the chest. I loved her strong will. I loved her fight. I loved that she never let me run over her.

I loved her.

Time, distance, space, or the world exploding couldn't change that.

"That's what scares the hell out of me."

Don't touch her. Don't touch her. Don't touch her.

But I couldn't keep my hand from grazing her forehead.

"Take pictures." Her throat bobbed as she swallowed.

It couldn't have been easy for her to ask that. But we needed evidence of the crime. I hoped she'd seriously consider putting him behind bars this time. Although I wasn't sure that was how the law worked for people of their stature. Could he just pay his way out?

I pulled my phone out of my pocket and snapped images of her injuries from several angles.

"My phone too. For back up."

Reluctantly, I backed away from her and grabbed her phone from the nightstand. The screen lit when I picked it up, revealing a text from Winston.

Replenish the ice.

He'd been the one with a level enough head to send her away with an ice pack.

I held up the device, and her eyes got glassy. I hadn't decided where the butler's allegiances lay, but he'd won some points with his behavior.

"Wanna unlock it for me?"

"The code is 0607."

My hand froze. June seventh. The day I'd ended things. I blinked at her.

"A reminder I never want to feel pain like that ever again," she said quietly.

Stab. Stab. Stab.

I'd hurt her to help her. But I'd never meant to cut her that deep.

I punched in the code and took the pictures again. When I was finished, she took the phone out of my shaking hand and blindly set it behind her.

She placed both palms on my chest.

I didn't want her to feel how my heart raced, but I couldn't control the tempo.

"I need you to make me a promise," she said. "A big one."

I'd already made big promises to her when she'd taken me as her husband. And I'd broken them.

"What is it?"

"That the only people you'll hold responsible for this are him and my father."

That was a massive promise to make.

I shook my head. "I can't."

I hated to say no to her, especially about something so important, but I didn't want to lie. I couldn't imagine a scenario where I'd ever get over the role I'd played.

"You can." She pressed her hands into me. "If you try."

"I'm sorry—"

"That's the last one of those too. Let's be done with apologies. What you've done for me says more than words ever could."

I stared into those dark eyes that controlled my soul.

She was right.

What I'd done did say more than words.

I'd failed her.

And in time, she'd see she shouldn't forgive me either.

CHAPTER TWENTY

BEAU

"THANKS FOR COMING WITH ME."

I linked arms with Lexie as we approached the county courthouse.

"I'm glad you asked." She nudged me. "This is the right decision."

The station had called Cal in to work half a shift for someone who was sick and he'd bolted like he'd been praying for an excuse to leave.

It hurt, but I understood.

As odd as it seemed, I felt more connected to him now than I had when we'd been together all those years ago. His guilt had become my own. As had his pain and burdens. They were heavy. And it would be a monumental task to beat all of it back.

But we would.

Or if I had to do it myself, I would.

I owed that to him.

"We could've done this at my office." Kane Zegas scowled as we entered the lobby. "I hate coming down here."

"From what I've heard, you'll charge me double." I smirked.

"Eh. Maybe I'll just put it on Elliott's bill." He grinned devilishly, as if the idea was genius.

"Maybe not. My debt to the Elliotts is racking up quickly."

Daniel and Vivian had given Teague, Pepper, Miss Adeline, and the dogs a place to stay. They'd opened their home to my entire family without hesitation. And they didn't seem to care if we ever left.

"I called in a favor with a judge I know to expedite the process. When you walk out of this building, you'll no longer be a Hollingsworth."

A sense of relief swept through me. At a time I hadn't thought it possible, hope bloomed.

I was almost free.

The night before had been the confirmation I hadn't wanted. My father had continually let me down no matter how many chances I gave him. I shuddered thinking about what could've happened if Cal hadn't been there.

He was the one who'd proved time and again I could count on him.

This was the right thing to do. What I wanted. Needed.

Lexie slipped her fingers in mine and squeezed. "So proud of you."

This felt like another step toward taking control of my life. A major one.

And when I'd told her my intention, she'd sent Lincoln and Eric off to make deliveries so she could support me. I could've easily asked my brothers to come, but I'd wanted my best friend.

Lexie had made sure to cover up my latest bruise by parting my hair a different way and creating a sweeping look over my forehead. Even if the makeup wore off, I was still covered.

A woman approached Zegas with a clipboard in hand. "The judge will see you now."

He made a grand gesture. "Lead the way."

Soon, so very soon, I'd have one piece of my past behind me.

"IT'S NOT FAIR."

Lexie handed me my temporary identification as we pushed out of the courthouse.

"No one should look that good in a driver's license picture, *Mrs. Calhoun.*"

I elbowed her, but couldn't help my grin. Without meaning to, Cal had given me such a gift.

"Has a nice ring, doesn't it?"

"It really does." She bumped shoulders with me. "Lincoln says your arrangement is a temporary fix. I'm not buying that."

Lexie knew me as well as anyone, even better than my friends in London. Sometimes that was a blessing and sometimes it was a curse.

"What makes you say that?"

"That man would walk through fire, a tornado, and barefoot on broken glass all at the same time for you."

I stumbled. When she put it in such blunt perspective, it was impossible to ignore. And while I wanted to argue, I wasn't sure I could.

"There's this intense energy when you two are in the same room," she continued.

I didn't bother to tell her that energy was there when we weren't too.

"It's . . . I don't know what," I said, at a complete loss for how to describe what was between Cal and me.

"You could start by defining temporary." She flashed me a sly grin.

I tried to glare, but it fell flat. "Beats the hell out of me."

"I was going to ask what happened between you two, but I'm pretty sure it's irrelevant now." Lexie was too smart for her own good.

Yesterday had been a defining moment for Cal and me. I'd found Garrett again. Any past hurt, any past decision he'd made to end things was completely obliterated. Because I finally understood that he was the most selfless and courageous man I knew. Lexie was totally right. I'd seen with my own eyes just what Cal was willing to do for me, and I had a feeling that was only the tip of the iceberg.

Except give you his heart.

That was the one thing I could grab on my own. Maybe he'd stolen mine, but I didn't want to do that. I needed him to want me because that was what he desired most. Not because he didn't have a choice.

"He took me to meet his mother."

Lexie's eyes widened. She understood the significance because she hadn't grown up in the greatest environment either. And I wished she and Eric would've been with me and devoured piles of lasagna.

Mrs. Calhoun—the older one—would have doted on them both as if they were her own children. I wanted that for my friends and my brothers.

I slung an arm around her shoulders. "Do you feel like getting into a little trouble?"

She rubbed her hands together. "If you were anyone else, I'd say it depends, but yeah, I'm down."

When we reached the bottom of the courthouse steps, I froze.

Parked across the street was a black sedan.

That asshole had a lot of nerve.

Had I really thought he'd stop following me?

CHAPTER TWENTY-ONE

CAL

I JOGGED up the stairs to Teague's apartment.

My building didn't have an elevator and I didn't want to get spoiled.

I reached the landing for his floor and hesitated. For a few minutes after work, I'd considered just going home. I'd even driven by. I'd thought about going to Ma's.

But I hadn't spoken to Beau since I'd left that morning. I needed to check on her. See that she was okay.

And I'd made vows.

I was still her husband. Pop would kill me if I didn't give it my all.

I pushed open the door to the apartment and stopped when the familiar scent of Ma's lemon chicken hit my nose. There was a herd of women and Eric surrounding her in the kitchen, which was a complete disaster.

Copper bolted toward me, followed by her puppies, but all the other dogs stayed in the kitchen, waiting for stray food to fall to the floor.

I quickly shut the door so the puppies didn't escape and knelt to greet them. "Hey, Mama. You and your babies are looking healthier."

She circled between my legs before leaning against one. The puppies circled my feet, all balls of energy.

My gaze was drawn across the room where dark eyes were on me.

Beau had flour on her cheeks and shirt. Her hair was piled on top of her head in a mess. And there was something in her look that scared me.

I'd only been afraid a handful of times in my life. When I'd carried Pop out of that burning building was one, and last night was another.

But this was a different kind of fear.

One I wasn't sure how to describe.

Something had changed in Beau. There was none of the hostility directed toward me anymore. I'd known what to do with her anger. It was easy to accept because I deserved it.

But this?

I didn't know what she was going to do.

"There's my baby boy," Ma said as if it had been years.

Teague snickered, and I glared at him. It felt just like home, only we were at his place. How did this happen?

"Baby boy, huh?"

I elbowed him in the ribs. He doubled over, pretending to be in pain.

"Hi, Ma." I kissed her cheek. "I'm starved."

"Of course you are. You don't eat enough." She picked up a spoon and dipped it in the sauce. "Eric, honey, does this taste okay?"

He leaned forward and she fed it to him. His eyes lit. "That's yummy. And we helped make it."

"You certainly did." She set the spoon down. "Does it have your stamp of approval for everyone else to eat?"

"Yes."

She turned off the stove. "Lincoln, Teague. Set the table please, boys."

I bit my lip to keep from smiling. Ma was in her element, cooking and directing everyone around like we were her little chicks.

They both moved to the cabinets. Teague handed Lincoln a stack of plates. I took a few glasses and Teague was right behind me with another handful.

"I'm not sure we have enough forks." Pepper worried her bottom lip between her teeth.

Ma patted her arm. "I brought some plastic ones just in case. And honey, I've probably lost more silverware than you've had in your life. That's what six boys will do." She pointed at me. "That one used to take my spoons and dig in the backyard."

My face got hot.

"I was planting some flowers not too long ago and found three of my grandmother's teaspoons," Ma said, but there was only affection in her voice. "Eric, you sit between me and Miss Adeline. Cal, will you take this platter to the table?"

"We only have six chairs," Pepper said as she moved to the table.

"Cal and Beau can share the ottoman and we can bring one of the barstools over. It will be a little high and low, but we'll all fit." Ma made taking care of people look easy.

I'm so damn lucky to have her.

And how the hell had she ended up here? I was glad to see her, but I hadn't put the pieces together yet.

I set the platter of chicken and pasta on the table, then pushed the ottoman over. Lincoln moved the barstool, while Teague set down two bowls of salad and a giant basket of bread.

I pulled Ma in for a hug. "Good surprise to see you here."

She hugged me back then swatted me away. "Let me serve everyone."

Once everybody had a mountain of food, and a few dogs beside them ready for any handouts, she grabbed Eric and Miss Adeline's hands. "Cal, say grace, please."

I took Beau's and Lexie's hands and cleared my throat before I said a quick blessing.

There was a moment of silence around the table, one that felt like gratitude for family. I didn't immediately let go of Beau's hand.

The bruise on her forehead peeked out from beneath her hair. If I focused on that, I'd trash the room, and now wasn't the time.

"You okay?"

"How was your day?"

We spoke at the same time. She giggled, drawing the attention of everyone at the table.

"You two have the strangest dynamic," Miss Adeline said. "Must be what makes you perfect together."

"Better watch out," Pepper said. She leaned her head on Miss Adeline's shoulder. "The old woman has a way of knowing things."

Miss Adeline swallowed a bite of chicken and pointed her fork at Ma. "I know that on the days Teague can't cook, you're coming over. Or we'll come to you. As long as you don't mind a bunch of dogs."

The woman didn't realize she'd just given Ma the best compliment in the world. Or maybe she did.

Ma beamed. "I'll cook for you whenever you like. And I expect to see all of you at my table in the Bronx."

"Mrs. Calhoun, thank you. This is delicious."

Everyone looked at Lincoln, except Beau. She smiled to herself. I guessed she was proud of her brother for being so kind to my mother. I appreciated it too.

"It's yummy, Mrs. C."

Ma piled more food on Eric's plate. His eyes went a little wide before he dug in.

"You don't have to eat all of that," I said before I pressed my lips together to keep from laughing.

"But you can if you want to, honey." Ma patted his hand.

Copper put her head on my lap, her nose inching toward my plate. I glanced around and held a piece of chicken in my palm. She smacked happily . . . and loudly.

Pepper lifted a brow at me.

"You're going to have to be quieter." I rubbed Copper's head.

She pawed my leg. Guessed it wasn't pets she wanted. It was chicken.

I held another piece of chicken out to her and she gobbled it up.

"Lexie makes amazing food for them," Pepper said. "Which they've already had tonight." Her tone was stern, but the twitch of her lips gave her away.

"Yet all these dogs want whatever we're having." Lexie scratched the side of her head, and everybody laughed.

Brutus edged his way over and stretched his face across Beau's lap, sniffing Copper.

"I've got you," Beau said quietly. She offered him a piece of her chicken.

He nudged it toward Copper.

My lips parted. I'd never seen a dog not inhale table food. But he seemed to want his—was she his girlfriend?—to have it.

Her tongue swiped across Beau's palm and it disappeared before he could change his mind. He sniffed her hand and smacked as if he were desperate for a taste. Beau tried again, and this time, he couldn't resist Ma's chicken.

He put his head in Beau's lap and she absently stroked his fur. That was another thing this apartment had that mine didn't. Dogs. And they were good for both of us.

Bites slowed down, groans began, and stomach rubbing commenced.

"We still have dessert," Ma said.

A collective moan went around the table.

"Can I save mine for a midnight snack?" Teague asked.

"You're all a bunch of lightweights," I said with a grin.

"I'd love some dessert." Beau picked up her empty plate, rounded the table to get Ma's, and dropped them in the sink.

"Of course you do, sweetheart. Help me get everyone a piece of cake."

"What kind is it?" I asked, taking my own plate to the sink.

She pinched my cheek. "Your favorite, chocolate."

When had she had time to bake a cake? She was like the Houdini of food, able to make a feast appear out of thin air.

Ma cut enough slices for everyone, even Teague, who dug in as soon as the dessert was in front of him.

He pointed with his fork. "I swear this is the best cake I've ever had. Will you leave some extra?"

"I'll leave the whole thing," Ma said. "What am I gonna do? Lug half a cake back to the Bronx?"

I snickered. "I'll keep an eye on it."

"More like keep your hands on it." She tilted her head and cut her gaze to Beau. "Although your hands are probably pretty occupied these days."

Miss Adeline high-fived her, then pointed a crooked finger at me. "You shouldn't have kept your mom away from us for so long."

I held up both hands. "I could hardly be in the presence of that one without getting lasered in half."

"Can we not talk about you touching my sister?" Teague complained grumpily.

Pepper swiped a glob of chocolate icing off his plate. "She had to endure hearing about us."

"She probably actually heard them," Miss Adeline said, motioning toward Lincoln and Lexie.

"Heard them doing what?" Eric asked innocently.

"Talking," Beau said quickly.

Lexie's face was bright red. Lincoln's was a shade lighter.

"You'll all come eat sometime when all my boys are over. I have a couple of folding tables I haven't used in a while. We could have a nice meal outside before it gets cold again." There wasn't hope or a question in Ma's tone. In her mind, it was decided.

"I love eating outside. Lincoln and I go to the park to eat hot dogs and donuts," Eric said, then clapped his hand over his mouth. "Oops."

Lexie slowly turned to Lincoln. "You've had hot dogs *and* donuts without me?"

"Ma, I'll give you a ride home," I said in an attempt to cool down the situation. It was hard to tell if Lexie was kidding or not. I was leaning toward not.

"I've got to do these dishes."

"No." Everyone spoke at once.

"You cooked, we clean," Teague said.

"If you're sure..."

"We're sure. Thank you, Mrs. Calhoun." Pepper hugged Ma.

That started the procession of goodbyes. Ma had to hug and kiss everyone twice, even the dogs.

"Let me take your purse," I said. It was more like a bowling ball bag that probably had enough supplies in it to survive an apocalypse.

"I'll ride with you," Beau said, right behind us.

Along with a dog whose name I didn't know. She whined and pawed at Ma.

"What is it, Ginger?"

"She doesn't want you to go," Miss Adeline said. "You could let her spend the night with you. We'll come get her tomorrow."

"I know how that goes," Lincoln muttered as he patted Muffy's head.

Ma looked longingly at the dog. "Oh, I don't know. I haven't had a pet in so long."

Ginger sat on Ma's feet. I had to hand it to the dog, she was convincing.

"I suppose one night won't hurt."

Pepper and Lexie jumped into action.

"Let me get a leash," Pepper said.

"I'll pack some food and treats," Lexie added. Sadie barked, and Lexie winced. "I said the T-word too loud, didn't I?"

"You could mouth it and that dog would hear." Miss Adeline rolled her eyes.

After a whirlwind, Ma had a leash in hand and Beau and I were loaded down with supplies.

"Good thing I have a big truck," I muttered.

Ginger's tail swished at a lightning pace as we rode down the elevator. Ma kept looking at her, almost with longing and uncertainty.

"You can sit up front, Mrs. Calhoun," Beau said when we reached the car.

I unlocked the tailgate and put everything in the back before helping Ma inside. Ginger jumped in after her.

"Oh goodness," she said as the dog sat on her lap.

Ginger was a big dog, though she'd been gentle on the way down.

"You okay?" Was she too heavy for Ma?

"Fine. Fine." She waved me off. "Just a little startled."

I patted the dog's head before closing the door. Beau had already climbed in the back seat.

"Ready to roll?" I fired up the truck.

Ginger licked Ma's face, and she laughed in a way I wasn't sure I'd heard since Pop passed. I hoped to hear more of it.

And one night? The only way that dog was coming back to Grey Paws was as a visitor.

CHAPTER TWENTY-TWO

CAL

"HOW DID ALL THAT COME ABOUT?"

I twirled my finger in the air as we pulled away from Ma's. Ginger had made herself at home, heading straight for the kitchen. It seemed the two of them were a perfect match.

"I stopped by and asked if she'd come cook for us," Beau said casually.

"You came here?"

"Believe it or not, they have this thing called GPS. You put in an address and voila." She kissed her fingertips.

I narrowed my gaze. "You shouldn't be wandering around alone."

One of those damn black cars had been at the station all day, and there was still one outside Ma's. But she still had security . . . and now Ginger.

"Lexie was with me."

Like that justified anything.

"The two of you shouldn't be out wandering alone. Did Lincoln know?" I gripped the steering wheel. Beau needed to take her safety more seriously.

"Neither of us need permission from him to go anywhere," she said tartly. "Or from you, for that matter."

"Damn it, Beau." I banged the dash with my fist.

She jumped. "We're fine. See?"

She motioned down her body, and yeah, she was fine this time. But her father clearly hadn't stopped stalking her. What if he made a move?

"You should at least let somebody know where you are," I growled.

She dug through her purse and retrieved her wallet along with a packet. "Here's where I was."

At a red light, she handed me a rectangular piece of paper.

A driver's license.

Beau Calhoun.

My stomach pitched. There it was. Legal.

And another invisible string tethered us together.

"I'm not giving your name back."

I jerked my head toward her. She was serious. I recognized that tone. The I*'ve made up my mind and there's nothing you can do about it* tone.

"Why?"

It was a stupid question. One I was pretty sure I wasn't ready for the answer to. And it was irrelevant. Because now that I'd been faced with it, I couldn't deny I wanted her to have my name too.

"I want a name I can be proud of. One that doesn't control me. One that represents the kind of family I always dreamed about."

She was proud to be a Calhoun? Wanted a family like mine? She worshipped her brothers. That couldn't have been an easy decision.

"If you'd have said that in front of Ma, she'd have cried."

"I'm not giving her up either," she said quietly.

My chest tightened. I wanted Beau to have a mother like mine, and I wanted Ma to have a daughter like Beau. But when she ended things, it was gonna be so damn hard it would break me.

I'd have to hold it together for them.

What about me, baby sister? Are you gonna give me up?

"I wouldn't ask you to."

"She was so good for everybody tonight." She fiddled with her gold chain.

"She was." I couldn't deny that. "Everybody was good for her too."

"I hope so." There was uncertainty in her voice.

"I know so."

She gently pried her identification out of my fingers and replaced it in her wallet. Then she took my hand in hers. "Zegas told me you talked to him about a post-nuptial agreement."

"Isn't there supposed to be attorney-client privilege?" I asked through my teeth.

He'd called me about Joe, but it bothered me that Beau wasn't protected. I wouldn't take anything that belonged to her, even if a court ordered it, but I wanted it on paper. To pay Zegas, I was going to have to take out a loan the size of New York City, but I'd figure it out.

Maybe Vigiano was right. It was time to think about a desk job. One that paid more.

And I needed to find time to at least grab a beer with my friend. I'd been too preoccupied lately.

"Garrett."

Why was she using my name now? Was she trying to wound me? Because it hurt. I'd been demanding she stop calling me Cal for weeks. Now that she had on occasion, I wasn't sure I could handle it.

"I don't want your money," I grated out.

"I know you don't," she said far too calmly for my liking. "But I'm not signing it."

"I'm trying to protect you." I stared straight ahead. "I won't take a penny."

"Don't get mad."

I braced myself. *What have you done, Beau?* "About what?"

"I paid Zegas today for Joe's defense."

"I had it worked out with him," I said, voice rising.

"Now you don't have to worry about it," she said coolly.

"It's my family. They're *my* responsibility."

She straightened. "They're my family too."

She'd never even met most of them. And this arrangement was

temporary. Why was she tangling it all up? Making it harder for me when she went back to London and left me behind?

I drummed the steering wheel with my free hand and couldn't make myself let go with the one she held.

The streetlights illuminated our joined hands on her lap every so often. Light. Dark. Light. Dark. Wasn't that how our relationship had been since she'd been back?

I drove aimlessly, though I hadn't headed toward Manhattan. When we passed by Mike's house, I realized maybe I hadn't been wandering after all.

"Everything I have is yours," I finally said. What was the point in hiding? Was I pretending not to feel for her sake or mine? I was failing miserably regardless of who I was doing it for.

"Except what I want," she said under her breath.

"*Everything.*"

If she didn't see that, I didn't know what else to do. And what could she possibly want that she didn't have? Especially from me.

"Can we go home now?"

"Let me drive by Bobby's, then we'll head back."

She looked out the passenger side window. "Someday I want to apologize to all of them. For what my father has done."

"You don't owe them an apology."

"I still want to." She turned up the radio.

"Good Time Charlie's Got The Blues" came on. She'd added it to this tape after I'd told her it was one of Pop's favorite songs. The music was painful and soothing at the same time. We'd listened to the song in his truck when I was a kid, and later when we'd ride to work together.

"YOUR MA CAN WHISTLE like this guy." Pop pointed to my radio.

"She can?" In all the times we'd heard this song, I didn't remember her ever whistling.

"Yeah. Did I ever tell you that's how I fell in love with her?"

I shook my head and looked across the truck at him.

"We were in junior high. I can't even remember who started the fight, but it turned into an all-out brawl."

I tried to imagine Pop in a rumble. He didn't back down from a fight, but I'd never seen him raise a fist.

"This ear-splitting whistle bounced off the gym walls. You know how it echoes in there."

I nodded. I did. It was awful off the concrete block walls.

"There she was. Standing at the top of the bleachers. She had on a blue dress and Coke-bottle glasses." He rubbed his jaw. "Donny landed a sucker punch to my face. Damn near broke my jaw. But I couldn't see anything but her."

"You knew her before that though, right?"

"Sort of. She was a couple of grades below me." There was a wistful look on his face. "I took those bleacher steps two at a time and told her she was gonna marry me."

He chuckled as if he were back in a memory a lifetime ago. "She pushed me and told me to get lost. I won her over with flowers and carrying her books around. Do you know how much shit a guy gets following a girl around like a puppy?"

Yeah. At one point, I'd dished it out to my buddies who'd gotten hearts in their eyes. And I'd definitely given a hard time to my brothers.

"How did I not know any of this?"

"Because your ma likes the version where I nearly crapped my pants asking her dad to take her on a date."

I couldn't imagine Pop being scared of anybody.

"Plus, she doesn't like to admit I was right. She married me, didn't she?" He smirked, but he didn't give a damn about being right or wrong. *He just wanted Ma happy.*

"You won."

"Luckiest bastard on the planet." He rolled down the window. "Someday a woman is gonna knock you for a loop. And when she does, you give her flowers every chance you get. It doesn't seem like much, but it makes up for the things you can't give her."

I tilted my head to the side. There were always fresh flowers at the house.

Didn't matter if Pop was dog-tired after a long shift, he never forgot Ma's flowers.

"I hated listening to my old man, especially now when I see how right he was about everything. But trust me. Flowers. She'll be yours forever."

HE'D TOLD me that not long before I'd met Beau. Looking back, I saw how right he was. Ma was his forever, but I wasn't sure if the flowers had anything to do with it.

Back when Beau and I had first gotten together, I'd been too scared to get her flowers. What if Pop was right and they made her mine forever? What if she was stuck with me?

Had anybody ever given her flowers?

The thought irritated me more than I cared to admit.

As I looked over at her pretty profile, part of our story was the same as my parents'. She'd knocked the daylights out of me from the minute we met.

I never dreamed she'd be my wife. The selfish bastard in me didn't care that it hadn't been all romance to get there.

And that damn question that kept rearing its ugly head sparked again.

What if I could keep her?

CHAPTER TWENTY-THREE

BEAU

"NOT MANHATTAN. *HOME.*"

I loved my family and all the chaos at Teague's. But I just wanted Cal.

His brows dipped, but he turned in what I hoped was the direction of his apartment. I hadn't gotten the reaction I'd hoped for when I showed him my new identification.

I hadn't realized how much I wanted him to be happy about it.

He hadn't seemed mad exactly, but . . . he wasn't glad.

It was like a wall had gone up between us after last night. He hadn't been as cold at dinner as I'd expected, but I felt the separation.

Hated it.

And I intended to erase it.

Because whether Garrett Calhoun knew it or not, I wasn't giving him up this time. I wanted his name, but more than that, I wanted his love. Because even though he suggested he'd never stopped loving me, he was questioning himself. He was wound so tight at the moment, so angry at himself. He'd saved me. He'd protected me from Alex's attacks. How could he blame himself?

What I felt for Garrett was the same as it had been all those years before. Love. I'd let him go before without a fight because I'd been blindsided and hurt. But only a fool wouldn't do everything she could to keep him. It had taken having my head rammed in a door to realize that, but no one ever said I wasn't hardheaded.

What I didn't know was if stealth was the best way to handle Cal or all guns blazing.

I hated to admit it, but I was scared. What if it was too late for us? What if I couldn't show him this was what we were destined for?

It had been a long, bumpy road to this point. Would I have truly appreciated Cal if we'd stayed together? I'd lived so much life since then. Learned so much about myself, about what I wanted. What I needed.

A few weeks ago, marriage hadn't been on that list.

Now, I clung to it with both hands.

If this isn't what he wants, will you let him go?

I couldn't think about that now. There were so many other hurdles to jump, and we'd take them one at a time.

When his building came into view, the relief was short-lived. A black sedan was parked out front. Cal tensed when he caught sight of it too.

"What's it gonna take to end this?"

I didn't move as he parked and turned off the truck. We sat in silence a moment.

"I have no idea."

He flicked his chin at me. "Then we'll just ride it out until it's over."

He was talking about my father, but did he also mean us? I was tired of guessing. Tired of having to tiptoe around.

I shoved out of the truck and marched over to the sedan. I tapped on the window not so gently. When it didn't roll down, I knocked harder.

The hum was short. A small gap revealed blue eyes and nothing more.

"Get out of here, or I'm calling the police for stalking me."

"It's not illegal to park on the street," he said coolly.

"It is if you're following someone."

"I'm sorry, ma'am, but I have no idea what you're talking about."

The window rolled up when I felt Cal at my back.

"Have it your way." I pulled out my phone. "Do you know the number to the police station?"

"I've got some buddies who can come down."

Cal murmured into his phone for a minute, and we went upstairs to the apartment.

He locked the door and pulled the curtain back on the front window. The sedan pulled away. Cal fired off a text to his police friends, I assumed to tell them the threat was gone.

"He could've had a gun." Cal tossed his phone on the coffee table.

"I've had enough."

I kicked off my shoes. They landed near the front door with a thud.

Cal watched them as if he'd never seen anything like it. Then I plopped on the couch and propped my feet on the coffee table.

"When is your next day off?" I asked.

"Day after tomorrow." He was still rooted in front of the TV, looking torn between joining me and running down the hall.

I wiggled my toes. The polish was chipped on my big toe, and I couldn't find it in me to care.

"I had some time to think about how to make this situation into something positive." I leaned my head back. "I thought I wanted to humiliate my father, but that's petty and ridiculous."

The sofa dipped when Cal sat beside me. He mimicked my posture, his boots landing on the wooden coffee table with a thud.

"What did you have in mind?"

"I . . . I just need you with me." I lolled my head toward him. "It's going to be hard, but it's important to me."

I couldn't crawl back in my shell and let this entire ordeal go to waste. I owed it to myself to find my bravery.

"I'm in."

No hesitation. No questions. Just unconditional support.

And I'd almost let this man go with my hatred.

I scooted closer and leaned my head against his shoulder. "Tell me something normal."

"You want a weather report?" His fingers drifted over to my thigh.

"Is it boring? If it is, that will do."

He snickered. "Thunderstorms with the possibility of hail and straight-line winds not what you had in mind?"

I groaned. "Is that really the forecast?"

"I have no clue. I just figure it out when I get outside. Or Ma calls and tells me to take an umbrella."

I lifted my head. "Does she really think you own an umbrella?"

One corner of his mouth turned up. "Apparently."

"She went on and on today about what all you've fixed for her lately." I smiled as I rested my head on him again. This was normal. Who we could be. A couple who just held each other and talked on lazy evenings. "You take care of her."

He shrugged, but he knew he did.

"You take care of everybody."

Especially me.

"I haven't done a very good job," he said bitterly.

"I beg to differ."

"All those damn fertility treatments, Joe's upside down on a house he's in jail for setting on fire. Aaron can't resist a bet. Mike drinks too much. Ben's wife is a good lady but wants stuff he can't afford. Bobby's got three kids close to going to college—"

His phone dinged with a text.

Need three hundred. I'll come get it.

Cal rubbed his temples with one hand. Whatever tension had evaporated since we'd been home returned with a vengeance.

"Damn it."

His fingers hovered over the screen, but he didn't type a reply.

He bolted from the couch and made purposeful strides down the hall.

The name above the text had been Aaron's. It didn't take much reading between the lines to figure out he needed more money.

I found Cal in the bedroom digging in the back of his top drawer.

He pulled out a canister and twisted the lid. When he shook it, only one bill came out. He peered inside and threw the container back in the drawer.

Then he moved to the closet, tossing a bag and some shoes out. He squatted and reached deep. When his arm reappeared, there was a worn velvet watch box in his hand. He opened it, lifted the white interior, and hurled it back into the closet.

"He promised he wasn't going to stay mixed up with these people." He hung his head. "I don't have it."

I touched his shoulder and he jolted as if he'd forgotten I was there. "What do you need?"

"For that damn bookie to stay the hell away from my brother," he growled. "Who am I kidding? He'd just find another one."

Slowly, he rose to his full height. Lines creased his face. The burden he bore was palpable.

He yanked on his hair and paced in a circle. "I'm enabling him. I know that."

"But he's your brother and you'd do anything for him."

Cal paused and blinked at me as if I'd given voice to his inner thoughts. If I were him, I'd do the same thing. It was all too easy to be on a high horse looking from the outside of a situation.

His phone chimed again.

He squeezed his eyes shut.

I slid my hands to his sides. "Do you want to give him the money?"

His eye lids flew open. "I'm not going to let you pay for his mistakes."

"There is no you and me anymore, Cal." I kissed his cheek. "It's we now."

"Not when it comes to money."

"I don't remember those vows excluding monetary resources."

He stiffened. "You didn't want to make them."

It was a low blow, although the truth. A truth I regretted. "But I did. You've stood by yours and I'm standing by mine. Now what do you want to do?"

The anger drained from his features. "I don't know what I'm

supposed to do."

Family was the easiest and most complicated thing in the world. Cal always knew what was best so it was weird to see him so conflicted.

"He has to decide to stop gambling. You can't do it for him."

He dropped his forehead to mine. "I know."

A tinge of pain shot through my skull, but I shoved it down. "What would your mom want you to do?"

He shrugged. "I'm afraid if I don't keep paying it off something bad will happen. Something worse than him owing the money. I can always try to make more of that. But I can't replace my brother."

"My father was right about the debt, wasn't he?" I hated to mention the man, especially in such a vulnerable moment. He'd made it sound as if Cal had been irresponsible, but I was beginning to see that wasn't the case at all.

He nodded.

Earlier Cal had rattled off where at least some of his money had gone, but I had a feeling that was only a fraction of what he'd done over the years.

"Just how big is your heart, Garrett Calhoun?"

His arms banded around my back. He was warm and solid and mine.

"I didn't want to worry Ma," he said hoarsely.

"You need to help him as a family. I've tried to go it alone. It doesn't work out so well."

He held me tighter. "I'll tell him to meet us at Ma's. You'll come with me, right?" He looked so hopeful I was pretty sure there wasn't anywhere I wouldn't go if he asked me to.

I cupped his cheeks. "Want me to drive?"

It was a bad time to joke, but I had to do something to loosen his tension.

He shuddered. "I'd rather go shopping in the women's department."

I slid my hand in his. "Be careful or you just might get what you wish for."

CHAPTER TWENTY-FOUR

CAL

"WHAT ARE all of them doing here?"

Aaron glared at me when he walked in the kitchen and saw all our brothers and some of their wives.

"You keep breaking your promise," I said calmly, keeping a hand on Beau's thigh for support.

"Who the hell is she?" He flicked his chin at Beau.

"Your family."

Bobby stood and pulled out his chair. "Sit down."

I recoiled. He sounded so much like Pop it nearly knocked the breath out of me.

Aaron glared at him too and wouldn't even look at Ma, who was seated in her spot at the head of the table.

"This has to stop," she said in that tone that had always scared the crap out of me. "You think it's fair to let your brother pay your gambling debt?" She pointed at me but kept her gaze locked on him.

He hung his head. "No."

"That should be reason enough for you to quit." She folded her hands on the table.

"I'm sorry." Everyone looked at me. I let out a long breath. "I should've told you no. Tried to find you help. I didn't do you any favors."

"It's not your fault," Aaron said incredulously, eyes wide. "I stopped keeping count of how much I owe you after it went over six figures." He dropped his chin to his chest.

Was it that much? I'd never kept a tab. There was no such thing when it came to them.

"You gave him over a hundred grand?" Ben asked in disbelief.

I lifted a shoulder and lowered it.

"Joe owes you at least that much for those damn fertility treatments. And you kept making payments on Ma's house after Pop died. I'm not even gonna get into what you've spotted me." He pointed at me.

Ma gasped.

"And me," Bobby said.

"And me," Mike added.

"This isn't about me." I focused on Aaron. "If I find you some help, will you take it?"

They had those phone numbers on casino commercials. There had to be somebody who could get my brother off this downward spiral.

I'd always managed to find more money to help him, but I was totally tapped out now.

And it wasn't fair to my wife.

She hadn't asked me for anything, but it wasn't just me to think about anymore.

"I'll get help." He rubbed his hands over his thighs.

"You're coming home where I can watch you properly," Ma said, leaving no room for argument.

"How much you owe?" Bobby asked, shoving Aaron's shoulder.

"Two grand," he said quietly.

"You told me three hundred," I said, voice rising.

"I got paid today, so I had some of it."

Mike smacked the back of his head. "You done being stupid?"

Behind the question was a boatload of worry we all felt. This wasn't a faucet that could be turned off. It was a long road that would be full of setbacks and starting over.

But we'd all be on it together.

"I'll try."

Ben smacked him too. "We love you, you dipshit." He grabbed him in a headlock from behind and rubbed his head.

"Watch your mouth," Ma said.

"Can I call him a dumbass?"

I rolled my eyes at Ben.

"Not in this house." Ma pointed. "Or outside of it."

She knew my smart aleck brother too well.

"I'm sorry," Aaron said quietly.

"We all make mistakes, baby. You just need your family to help you through them." Ma stood and pulled him out of his seat for a hug.

He clung to her like he was a kid instead of a grown man. But sometimes we just needed our ma.

Beau squeezed my thigh.

I kissed the side of her head.

"So, when you gonna introduce us to our new *family*?" Bobby asked, pointing his head at Beau.

There hadn't been time for any of that before Aaron arrived.

I cleared my throat. "This is Beau."

"What are you doing with an idiot like him?" Ben asked, grinning.

"She's way out of your league," Mike chimed in.

"Your wife is out of your league too," Michelle chimed in, linking arms with my brother. "Just like I'm out of Bobby's." She turned her attention to Beau. "Welcome to the jungle. I'm Michelle. This big lug's wife." She elbowed Bobby.

Beau looked a little overwhelmed but managed to find her voice. "Nice to meet you, Michelle. All of you really."

"You are so screwed, dude," Ben said. "If you fu—" He looked at Ma. "F this up, I'll kick your ass."

"He already did," Mike said.

How'd he know? Did he suddenly have a fortune-telling gift I didn't know anything about?

"I hate to argue, but no, he didn't," Beau said.

Brows went up around the kitchen. Beau held her chin up.

Bobby smirked. "She fits in around here."

"Don't you boys give her a hard time," Ma said. "You know I want more daughters." She narrowed her gaze at Mike who held his hands up.

"I can't handle any more kids, Ma."

"You only have two," she pouted.

"Point made."

"He thought we didn't know he was sneaking off way back when. I saw you two going up to the station house rooftop all the time." Mike gave me a triumphant look.

"Is this the broad you were doing that with?" Bobby asked. "We wondered what happened to her."

"Is nothing sacred around here?" I grumbled.

"You should've introduced us back then. Maybe you wouldn't have screwed it all up," Ben said.

I couldn't argue. Didn't want to.

"I'd love to see the groveling you had to do to get her back." Bobby thumped me on the head.

Michelle thumped him. "I wish you would so you could take a lesson." She squeezed Aaron's shoulder. "You good for now? We need to get back to the kids."

"I'm good."

"Call us when you need us." She hugged him.

I stood and Beau did the same.

Michelle embraced us both, along with everyone else until only Ma, Aaron, Beau, and I remained.

"Cal . . ." Ma said carefully in that voice that made me want to shrink to the floor. "Did you pay off this house?"

I stared at my feet. It had taken me until last year, and every time I made one of those payments, it eased a little of my worry about Ma, knowing she was taken care of.

"Garrett Calhoun, you answer me this minute." Her hands were on her hips now.

"I needed to do it. For you. And Pop," I said quietly.

"That's not your responsibility, baby boy." She reached for my hand.

"He took care of all that stuff. I didn't want you to worry about it."

"Don't you dare tell me you've been paying the light bill, the insurance, and everything else."

I clamped my mouth closed in obedience. I hadn't wanted her to know. Pop had been the one to take care of the bills. Ma was perfectly capable, but I needed to do it. In a weird way, it made me feel closer to him.

"How much, Cal?"

"Doesn't matter." I pulled her in for a bear hug.

"A mother is supposed to take care of her boys," she protested. "You could've bought your own house or whatever you wanted."

"You do take care of me. And I did what I wanted."

She looked up at me with watery eyes. "Promise you won't do it anymore."

"Can't do that," I said quietly.

She patted my back. "What am I going to do with you?"

"Keep feeding me. And keep me in line."

She grinned. "I can do that. Let me get my wooden spoon."

Beau and Aaron snickered.

Ma released me after one more squeeze and pinched Aaron's cheek. "Young man, we are going to get you straightened out."

Judging by the determination in her tone, she would. Because I knew Ma. While it wasn't her fault Aaron had made poor choices, she blamed herself. And she wouldn't stop until he never gambled again.

"Thanks, Ma. Cal." Aaron's gaze was troubled, and it might take a while for him to forgive me for calling in the whole family, but one day he'd be okay.

"See you tomorrow," I said.

Beau gave them both a quick hug before we went to my truck.

As soon as we were both inside, she twisted in her seat to face me. How many times had she done that when we were kids? I'd loved it then, and I loved it now.

"Do you feel like you did the right thing?"

I tapped the wheel for a second. "I think so. I guess time will tell."

"You called me family."

"Don't look so shocked." I brushed her hair back from her forehead. That bruise was nasty. I hoped wherever that bastard was he was in a lot of pain.

"Are you sure you want me to get used to it?"

The question was loaded. A bomb a half a second away from detonating. What I wanted and what I could have weren't necessarily the same thing.

I cranked the engine, threw it in drive, and touched her knee. I'd feared her seeing my family dynamic and thinking we were all just hoodlums. But she'd laughed and encouraged and offered silent support throughout the whole night, and I was in awe. And she wanted more of it. More of us.

More of me.

Was I sure I wanted her to get used to it? Absolutely.

"Not sure I have a choice, baby sister. Not sure I have a choice."

CHAPTER TWENTY-FIVE

BEAU

"I THOUGHT the point of us staying in one building was better protection."

Lincoln crossed his legs and wrapped his hands around his knee.

"It doesn't work that way if you and Cal are somewhere else."

I flopped on Teague's sofa next to him. "Are you the safety patrol now?"

He scowled and I kissed his cheek, which immediately softened him.

I looked around. The apartment was a little messy, but quiet. Too quiet. "Where is everybody?"

"Downstairs. Lexie insisted I see about *my empire* for a few hours this morning." A smile teased his lips.

"Have I told you how happy I am for you?" I slipped off my shoes and tucked my legs under me.

"I didn't know it was possible," he said, almost in awe. "To feel . . . so much."

He was lucky. He'd never have to experience the other side of that coin. The painful one.

"I think the dogs are the most shocking part of the whole thing." I grinned.

"It is rather surprising. In fact, it's a bit too quiet around here now."

I hugged a throw pillow. "I couldn't sleep last night. I've tried to come up with a solution about the company. I just can't."

If it weren't for the employees, I'd walk away and never look back. Lincoln would understand. He might even walk with me.

But I bore a responsibility to these people.

"It's . . . delicate."

I snorted. That was one way of putting it. "More like disaster." I hugged the pillow harder. "If we could just get rid of him—"

"I meant what I told him. Zegas drafted a letter demanding he sign over your portion of the company within three days."

I straightened. "What do you have on him?"

He slumped. "Nothing really. I'm hoping my bluff will at least scare him into giving you and Teague what belongs to you."

"And what about what belongs to you?"

He shrugged. "It's more important to me that you two are taken care of."

I whacked him with the pillow. "I'm more than fine without the company."

"I'm aware. But it belongs to you and you'll have it."

"Do you think he had Mom killed?" I asked quietly.

"No." He rubbed his jaw. "But he knows who did it. My guess is he's exacted his revenge."

"Did he give you and Teague anything the other night? Something of Mom's?" There was a desperate edge to my voice. I wanted *something* of hers. Anything that would tell me about her.

"She loved you," he said hoarsely. "She'd tease me about how I watched over you, but she never let you get too far out of her sight."

"Was I . . . there?" I swallowed hard.

"No." His eyes rounded. "She and Winston argued about who was going to the deli. He never raised his voice, but that morning, he was . . . almost like he was panicked. I'd forgotten that."

"You don't think . . ." The man had taken care of us, been there for us. Could he have been involved in her murder?

"I can't imagine it."

I dropped my head back and stared at the ceiling. "It doesn't matter if Father's dead or we never see him again. He's always going to loom over us, isn't he?"

"Not if I can help it."

The front door burst open. "Just the two Hollingsworths—I mean Hollingsworth and Calhoun—I wanted to see."

"I thought this building was secure," Lincoln grumbled as Kane Zegas made himself at home in a club chair beside us.

"All access, baby." He pulled a folder out of his briefcase. "Believe it or not, your old man responded to our little letter. I have to say, I'm stunned." He thumbed through the file. "Actually, I'm not. I am a master at composing threatening letters."

"Ego much?" I asked.

"If you wanted a mouse for an attorney, go hire Whitley."

"Did I hear my name?" The other man sauntered into the apartment. "I promise you want me at this party."

"Before you begin, let me phone Teague. He should be here." Lincoln reached for his phone at the same time our brother appeared.

"I'm the best because I know what you need before you do," Zegas said.

"The best? Psh." Whitley rolled his eyes. "I'm going first. My update is by far more interesting than yours."

Zegas wrinkled his nose. "If pretending to assert your dominance makes you feel better—"

"Gentleman, can we get on with this?" Lincoln growled.

I scooted to the middle of the sofa to make room for Teague. Flanked between my brothers, I felt ready for anything.

Whitley shoved a pair of glasses on his face.

"Are those for looks?" Zegas asked. "They don't make you appear more intelligent."

Whitley cleared his throat as if annoyed and shook out the paper in his hand with a flourish. "Have you ever considered returning the stalking favor to your father? He's been quite the busy man."

I tensed. Maybe I wasn't ready for anything. Did I want to know what he did on a daily basis? And had Lincoln asked them to tail him?

"As long as he leaves us the hell alone, I don't give a damn what he does." Teague folded his arms over his chest.

"Do you really believe he's going to do that?" I asked.

"No," he grumbled.

"He visits your mother's grave every morning and evening," Whitley said.

It might as well have been a slap. Those were the actions of a man who loved his family. How could my father have never stopped mourning Mother yet treated his children as he did? It was as if he blamed us somehow for losing her. Or . . . I couldn't begin to understand the mindset of a madman.

"Is that supposed to make him human?" I muttered. "Maybe you're mistaken and he's using another spot in the cemetery as the portal to hell."

Zegas snorted. "Good call."

"I haven't figured out any pattern to which of you he follows at a particular time, but it's a pretty even split," Whitley continued. "We've even found your detail in London, Beau. So far it consists of three people, all ex-MI6."

"Like the intelligence agency?" I asked incredulously.

"Yes."

I threw my hands up but caught the throw pillow before it fell. "What is wrong with him?"

"I was going through some of my father's things over the weekend," Zegas said. "I found notes from his investigation back then. He mentioned there was a security detail on all of you at all times. What we don't know is if this started before or after your mother's death."

"Did you find anything else in those files?" Lincoln appeared almost eager.

I thought I'd been alone in my quest for knowledge about Mom. Maybe my brothers were just better at hiding their curiosity.

"Nothing more than generic case crap." Zegas seemed disappointed he hadn't struck gold in the information department.

"A couple of nights ago, he had Alex Davenport admitted to a private medical facility."

I shot up from the sofa. He'd seen to that asshole's medical care, but couldn't be bothered with his own daughter's?

"How much worse does this get?" I asked through my teeth. "Because I'm not sure I'm equipped to handle it."

I touched my forehead to the floor-to-ceiling glass windows and hissed. I'd forgotten about my head, but it was another cruel reminder of just how little I meant to my father.

"The thing is, Alex never left that facility." Whitley tilted his head. "But he's no longer there."

"How do you know that?" I seriously doubted anyone could walk into a place like that and inquire about patients.

"It's sad, yet completely understandable what a little cash can do. One of the nurses assigned to him said he was there when she left her shift and gone when she returned the next morning."

"I'm sure patients come and go frequently," Lincoln said.

"Not ones in a coma."

I wheeled around. "A coma? He was conscious when we left."

"The nurse got all shifty until we flashed more cash," Whitley said. "She said he had a hell of a bruise on his forehead. His skull was fractured, like he'd had his head rammed into a door or a wall."

I clutched my chain and looked back and forth between my brothers, who appeared as stunned as I was.

"The Davenports filed a missing persons report this morning," Zegas said.

"Is he... dead?" And was I a horrible person for the part of me that felt some relief at that?

Whitley shrugged. "We don't know. But I'd say it doesn't look good for the guy."

"Can you get proof our father had something to do with his disappearance?" Lincoln's knuckles were white where he clasped his knee.

"The truth? It's unlikely," Whitley said. "We only know of your father's involvement because we have eyes and ears on him twenty-four seven. But he's good at keeping his distance. The car that transported Alex is registered to a limo company. The money came in an envelope. We could put the cops on his trail, but they can't use our methods."

"And he has people on the inside," Teague said in disgust. "That investigation would probably be over before it started."

"My concern is that he may try to frame Garrett Calhoun for Alex's disappearance." Zegas tossed his pen on the coffee table.

"No." The word was out of my mouth before I thought.

"Based on what you've told me about the events of the evening you last spoke to your father, I'd say it's possible that was the intention. Samuel knows Mr. Calhoun's feelings for you, probably better than he does himself. He was well aware of the potential consequences of having you, Alex, and Calhoun in the same space."

I shook my head, ignoring the throbbing in my skull. "Garrett did nothing wrong. He likely saved my life." My voice trembled. "None of you were there. You don't know what Alex was like. What he was going to do."

I folded my arms over my stomach and tried to curl in on myself as that helpless fear threatened to drown me. He was going to rape me. I was certain of it.

Teague and Lincoln surrounded me. I closed my eyes and tried to draw calming strength from them. It helped a little, but I needed someone else.

I needed Cal.

"If Dad killed him, it's the best thing he's done in a long time."

I snapped my head up toward Teague. He wasn't a violent guy and was usually levelheaded. Definitely more easygoing than Lincoln and me.

"I don't mean that lightly."

Teague was so good with the dogs and Pepper and Miss Adeline. He valued life. Was forgiving . . . except with our father.

Lincoln kissed the side of my head. "I'm not sorry to say that I agree with Teague."

"We can't let him frame Cal," I whispered.

As much as I wanted to believe Zegas and Whitley were grasping at straws, they weren't. What they'd said made sense. It fit Father's agenda.

If I wouldn't get rid of Cal, he would. Just as he said he would. He'd ruin him any way he could.

CHAPTER TWENTY-SIX

CAL

BEAU SPRINTED toward the door and flung herself in my arms as soon as I stepped into Teague's apartment.

"That's a hell of a way to welcome a man home," I murmured against her hair when I caught her.

She buried her face against my chest and held me so tight I could hardly breathe.

I stroked her hair. "Hey. What's this about?"

Worry wound its way through me. Beau was affectionate, though it had been more reserved when it came to me lately, but this . . . this was a lot. Especially in front of her family.

"We think my father killed Alex and is going to frame you," she wailed.

My relief yo-yoed to *what the hell* in a nanosecond.

"That's not going to happen. I'm innocent," I said far more calmly than I felt.

Her father was capable of anything, including framing a peon like me for murder.

But we had a justice system. I was a dedicated employee of the city, came from a family of decorated heroes. That had to mean something, didn't it?

I hooked her chin. Those dark eyes were tumultuous with fear and anger and worry.

"Let's take a walk."

I grabbed two leashes off the closet door handle. Copper trotted closer, like she knew a leash was meant for her. Brutus was more hesitant but let me loop the leash around his neck.

I held both with one hand and ushered Beau out of the apartment with the other on the small of her back. She tucked herself in my side and took Brutus's leash. He sat on her foot once we were in the elevator, while Copper pressed against my leg.

Once we were out in the evening air, we wandered at a slow pace toward the park.

"I'm sorry I blurted all that out the second you came home," Beau said. She'd stayed close, but we were no longer touching.

"Just a day in the life, right?"

She stared at me incredulously. "How can you be so casual about this?"

"I pulled a woman and her two kids out of a fire today," I said quietly. "A few minutes later . . ." I couldn't finish the sentence. "Kinda puts things in perspective."

She stopped. "Are they okay? Are *you* okay?"

"Everybody is fine." I touched her elbow, encouraging her to keep moving. "It's my job, Beau."

She let out a long breath. "I know. But somehow I've concocted this image about what you and Teague do all day. It includes cooking, washing fire trucks, and calendar shoots."

"If only it were that glamorous." I smirked.

She elbowed me in the arm.

"I have washed more fire trucks than I care to count," I said.

"Shirtless?" One side of her mouth quirked up.

"You like thinking about that?"

She'd fired a cannon at me when I'd walked through the door, and in typical Beau fashion, she'd made me forget everything else but her . . . and made me smile in the process.

"Not feeding your already large ego." She lifted her chin.

"Do you think I have a big ego?"

"No, but it was better than admitting I plotted out an entire calendar shoot of you shirtless washing fire trucks. And dogs. That would sell like hot cakes." She let out a low whistle.

Brutus looked back as if unsure what he was supposed to do.

"Ain't happening."

Copper bolted toward a squirrel, dragging me along with her. Brutus joined in the chase. They barked at the base of a tree while the squirrel taunted them from a high branch.

I squatted between them and tried to settle them. "You got him."

They finally stopped barking.

When I stood, Beau had a look in her eyes that nearly sent me to my knees. She wasn't hiding anymore. I should've known that the minute she rocketed at me earlier.

I'd seen that look before. The first time I'd taken her to the fire station roof. And every time after that.

Now it was more intense. Because there was more between us. Things that had fused us together whether we meant for them to or not.

"We should keep going." I flicked my chin toward the squirrel. "Before he decides to pelt me with acorns."

"Acorns?" She shook her head. "You're nuts." Then she covered her mouth with her hand to stifle her laugh. "I didn't mean to do that."

Which made it all the funnier.

Damn, she was beautiful when she smiled. When she wasn't hiding her heart from me.

"You've never had a squirrel throw acorns at you?" I asked as if she were the crazy one.

"No. And you haven't either."

I held up one hand. "I swear on Engine 42. Richman Park. The little suckers pelt people with them."

"You're lying."

"You don't believe me?" I moved ahead. "Fair warning. Bring a hard hat. Maybe some goggles."

Her laughter was the best sound I'd ever heard. "I'm looking forward to proving you're making this up."

"Suit yourself." I shrugged. "And when I'm not, I get the last piece of Ma's Italian cake on Sunday."

My steps faltered. I'd just talked about family plans like it was a given she'd go. Like we'd been going to dinner at Ma's for years.

"How do you know she's baking Italian cake?"

I grinned. "I asked her to."

She made a face. "Soon it isn't only going to be the squirrels pegging you with acorns. And that piece of cake is mine."

"Not a chance. Isn't that right, Copper?"

She looked back at me like I was an idiot. Maybe I needed another woman to put me in my place.

"Even she knows you're full of it." Beau bumped me.

I bumped her back.

We were acting like we were fifteen instead of going on forty. And it was so nice, I wanted to walk in this park until we dropped.

"My legal counsel has advised against me doing what I planned for us tomorrow," she said.

But what she didn't say was she didn't care. I heard it in every syllable.

"Still in."

"Why do you do that?"

"What?" I lifted a shoulder and lowered it.

"Say yes to anything without asking what it is first," she said in disbelief.

"Figure you wouldn't ask if it wasn't important." *Haven't you realized I can't say no to you?*

She stopped in the middle of the sidewalk. Brutus looked torn between staying with her and following Copper and me.

"Why did you push me away?" she asked quietly.

I looked away. She didn't have to say when. The pain in those eyes had haunted me every night until she'd come back into my life.

"You're like standing next to the sun."

She looked at me with . . . awe at my comment. She was bright and beautiful and fire. How could she not see that?

But then a cloud came over her expression.

"It was my fault." She hung her head, and I couldn't take it.

I stepped into her space and cradled her jaw. "No, it was mine. I wasn't good enough for you, and I damn sure wasn't going to hold you back."

Her expression went from shocked to anger. "How would you hold me back?"

"You had everything ahead of you. I was as far as I'm ever going to go. You deserved to fly."

I hated it had to be that way, but I'd never regret it.

Her eyes flashed. "I needed you." She erased the small distance between us. "Do you think I'd choose business over you?"

"What about the friends you made over there? The life you built?" I challenged.

"I love them. And I love the life I have. But I loved you more than all of it combined."

Stab.

She slashed me open and drained me out. I'd been lucky enough to have a lot of people care about me. But they were family. Obligated in a way.

Those weren't just words. It was on her face, in her posture, coming off her in waves.

She'd have chosen me.

"And I loved you enough to let you go."

"You took the easy way out." Her voice was low and dark.

"Easy? Baby sister, that nearly killed me. I'm still not over it." The confession tumbled out before I could stop it. I'd tried to keep a lid on my feelings for her sake. If she thought I didn't care, she'd forget about me a lot quicker.

Her lips parted.

I couldn't understand why what I'd said would be a surprise to her. I'd said some awful things way back, but even when I'd become her booty call, I'd never treated her like an object. Like I did anything less than care about her.

She shoved a finger in my chest. "You stole from us. We lost years, Garrett."

Maybe she was right. But I did what was best for her.

I clamped my mouth shut. I'd already said too much. We didn't get a redo.

She dug her finger in the spot above my heart. "Great. Stand there. Pretend like it doesn't matter." She turned her head. "I guess that's better than you spouting off hurtful things like you did back then."

"I lied."

She jerked her head back toward me. I nodded.

"It's the only successful lie I've ever told."

Her face twisted in pain. "You made it sound like the truth."

My chest heaved. "Be sure you know what you want this time. Because I don't have it in me to do it again."

CHAPTER TWENTY-SEVEN

BEAU

SILENCE.

Sometimes it was nice.

Sometimes it was not.

Cal and I hadn't said a word to each other since our walk. Not when we'd gotten into bed. Not when he'd slung an arm around me. Not when Copper had jumped on the mattress and Brutus had dragged the basket of puppies into our room.

The morning hadn't started any different.

We'd gotten ready in silence.

But he'd taken my hand when we'd left our room and had only let go while we loaded in his truck.

"I can't take the silent treatment anymore."

He flipped on a turn signal. "I figure if I don't say anything, I can't screw things up any worse."

My heart squeezed. "I'd rather argue with you than not talk at all."

He cut his gaze to me before returning it to the street. If that statement didn't tell him my intentions, what I wanted, I'd have to spell it out.

We crossed the Willis Avenue Bridge over the Harlem River. Were we headed to his apartment? His mother's? To see Joe?

Do you really care?

No, I didn't.

I turned up the radio and grinned at the song playing. He smirked when I held up a fist microphone and began to sing "Respect Yourself" by The Staple Singers at the top of my lungs.

He stuck his finger in his ear. "Silence. I'll take the silence."

I pretended to whack him over the head with my microphone, but kept right on singing.

The person in a car we passed looked at me like I was crazy, but I didn't care. As I belted out the words, the truth hit me.

I wasn't going back to London.

Even if the unthinkable happened.

I'd miss my friends there, but that's what planes were for. I'd miss my colleagues. I'd miss seeing what I'd built.

I devoted a lot of years to those things, and they'd always be part of me. But it was time to be selfish. To focus on what I truly wanted. Not my father. Not my brothers. Not those I felt obligated to.

A page had turned in my life.

I needed the people here for this chapter.

Abruptly, I stopped singing.

"Garrett?"

"I owe you a better honeymoon than a diner." He wheeled into the parking lot of the Bronx Zoo. "Do you want to start with camels or ice cream?"

I clutched my mother's chain. She had to have sent this man to me. There was no other explanation.

My nose got tingly and my eyes stung. "Ice cream. Then camels. Then bears. Then more ice cream." My voice was scratchy with emotion.

"I'm not getting in the bear exhibit."

I giggled. "Good. I'd hate to have to call your mother."

He shuddered before he jumped out of the truck and opened my door.

I grabbed his big hand and dragged him toward the entrance. "No one's ever had a better honeymoon."

"We haven't even seen the camels yet."

"Doesn't matter."

Garrett listened to me. There was nothing he did that didn't have my happiness in mind. And I prayed I could do the same for him.

Just before we reached the ticket office, I stopped.

"I'm paying," he said gruffly.

I threw my arms around him and smashed my lips to his. Fire blazed through me at the feeling of his mouth on mine. This. His lips. His kiss. It was what I'd missed probably more than anything else. The connection I'd only ever known through kissing this man. He was the only person I'd ever kissed. The only one who made me feel so much it was too much and not enough at the same time. And I wanted him to know all of that in this kiss. That he was and would always be the one I wanted. Just him.

Startled, it took him a second to catch up, but when he did, his return kiss was starved. Garrett had held the pieces of my heart this entire time and hadn't even realized it. He wrapped his arms around my back and held me like he'd never let me go.

He kissed me as if he'd never get enough.

Everything disappeared but him.

I'd spent so much time hating him. I'd stolen from us too. Because if I'd have let it go, we could've had this.

Although, now his lips on mine were even better than I remembered. I appreciated him because I knew what it was like to be without him. There was so much sizzle and spark and something powerful I thought I'd be consumed on the spot.

He put his forehead to mine, breaths shallow. "I thought you only kissed people you love."

"I do."

"Hell, Beau. I love you too. I never stopped."

Words I'd needed to hear. Needed to soak in to heal my brokenness.

"So, will you stop thinking you're not enough, please? It's only ever been you, and it will only ever be you."

He took my lips again in affirmation, this time with even more determination and lust. Finally. Home. "I'll try. For you."

I smiled and reached up and kissed him one more time. Because I could.

I pulled him toward the ticket line and he followed me in a daze. But it didn't take long for him to be back in command.

He moved with purposeful strides to the first ice cream cart we saw.

"I should know what flavor you like," he said more to himself than me.

"Cookies and cream."

He ordered for both of us and offered me a cone.

"Did we ever have ice cream?" he asked as we wandered toward a bench.

"I don't think so." I licked a taste and hummed. "Why did I ever give up sugar?"

"You don't eat sugar?" he asked as if I'd told him the sun was never coming out again.

"Believe it or not, before I came back to New York, I hadn't had any in . . . two, three years maybe."

"Don't tell Ma that," he said. "She'll have a heart attack." Then he flashed me a sly smile. "Actually, you just keep right on not eating sugar. I'll suffer through eating all her desserts."

I narrowed my gaze. "That piece of Italian cake is mine. I don't even know what it is, but I'm having it."

He smirked. "Not this round. You shouldn't doubt me about these squirrels."

My face nearly cracked, I was grinning so wide. Garrett looked years younger, like he'd let go of some of that weight he carried. I wanted to keep it that way. Share the load so he wasn't all alone.

And I didn't mean financial load, although I was still in shock from how much he'd been looking after his family all these years. My father was critical of him, thought Cal beneath him. But a man who looked after his family, even to his own financial detriment, was extraordinary, not a man deserving of my father's scorn. Or anyone's for that matter. No, I had been right all those years ago about Garrett Calhoun, and I was right now. He was worth any sacrifice. And he was mine.

I popped the last piece of cone in my mouth. "I'm ready for camels."

He scarfed the rest of his ice cream down. "Let's go find some to feed."

"BABY SISTER, we can't take him home. He won't fit in the apartment."

I hugged Aldo one more time. We'd done something better than feeding camels. We'd ridden them.

"But we're friends now," I protested.

"Even if he spits in your face?" Garrett laughed.

"Even if he spits in my face."

"Do you want to ride him again?"

I looked at the line of children waiting their turn. "No. Maybe another time."

We exited the exhibit and Aldo followed us to the edge of the enclosure.

"He wants to come with us."

Garrett's expression turned serious and he dropped to one knee.

I clutched my necklace.

"Marry me. Not because you have to but because you want to."

My heart pounded in my chest. I stared down at the only man I'd ever loved. Kindness. Compassion. Generosity. Love. Loyalty.

All of it looked back up at me.

He dug in his pocket and pulled out a simple diamond ring. "It belonged to my grandmother."

I hit my knees and cupped his face. "Yes. Yes. Yes. Yes."

His face lit like I'd just given him the best gift ever.

He slid the ring on my finger. "I love you. Always have. Always will."

I looked down at the diamond. It sparkled in the sunlight. This ring had meant something to his family. And now I was part of that.

"Don't try to leave me again," I whispered.

"Didn't you hear me last night? I don't have it in me to do it a second time." He brushed his lips across mine. "You thought we'd get a divorce when this was done. But I never had any intention of letting you go."

I kissed him long and hard and fierce, with everything I had.

Garrett Calhoun was mine.

And for the first time in eleven years, I felt whole.

CHAPTER TWENTY-EIGHT

CAL

"OLIVIA SAID we could park in the alley."

"You aren't healed. I can't touch you." I wanted to though. "And who's Olivia?"

Beau rolled her eyes. "The owner of the hotel. I like this place. I talked to her about buying it."

I shook the cobwebs out of my head. Would I ever get used to the fact that my wife could pretty much buy anything she wanted and not even notice a dent in her bank account?

I rolled past the hotel on West 56th. I wasn't keen on it, not because the place wasn't nice. But the last time I'd met Beau here, she'd been hurt.

Was that asshole really dead?

"Right there. Next to the cake van. That's where she said to park." Beau pointed at a hot pink van that nearly blinded me.

I wheeled in where she directed and turned off the truck. "Did your lawyer advise against you sleeping with me?"

Beau folded her hands in her lap and looked down at them. She tried to smile, but it was hollow. "I didn't discuss our sex life with him."

"You can tell me why we're here or I can be surprised. But don't ask me to do something I can't."

Now that we'd ripped the lid off of everything, that we knew we were both here because we wanted to be, it was that much harder for me not to show her how I felt with my body.

We were closer than we'd ever been and that physical connection was another form of expression I wanted to share with her again.

Beau could be persuasive when she wanted to be, although it didn't take much convincing on her part when it came to me. I wasn't saying no to her. Just later.

She drew in a deep breath and released it as if she were mentally counting backward from ten. "I wish we were here for that, but we're going to the ballroom. It's the only open space Olivia had available today."

"You know I can't dance."

This time her small smile was genuine. "We're not dancing either." She pulled on the door handle. "Let's go before I lose my nerve."

She punched in a code near the back door and the lock clicked.

I held it open but caught her hand as she passed. The diamond ring flashed. Mine.

I hadn't realized how badly I needed my ring on her finger. But my left ring finger burned. I needed to be hers too. To have that reminder that this was real. Permanent.

"I've got you," I said.

"I know." She pecked my lips.

Every time she kissed me, it was an *I love you,* and I'd never get enough. It was better than the words.

I was the same guy I'd always been. The one who loved my family, my job, and her. But since she'd left, I'd been a shell of that guy.

She'd given me my life back.

I'd never believe I deserved her. Nobody did. But I meant what I told her. I wasn't strong enough to let her go again.

"That cake needs more sprinkles." A woman behind the front desk put her hands on her hips.

"We already used two bottles on it." Another woman tugged on her apron. "Who's the professional baker here? Me or you?"

"Hi, Olivia," Beau said with a raised brow.

"Beau. Hey." The lady in the dress who wanted more sprinkles hurried around the desk. "I have everything set up for you. Follow me." She walked backward and pointed at the lady in the apron. "More sprinkles, Roxy. You know I'm right."

The woman groaned. "You want more sprinkles, I'll give you more sprinkles."

"Everything okay?" Beau asked as we walked across the lobby.

Olivia waved her hand absently. "That's just my best friend. You'd think by now she'd realize I'm always right."

"I heard that," Roxy called.

"And apparently she has supersonic hearing." She moved at a quick clip like time was short and too important to waste. "No one else has arrived yet."

Beau stopped. "I should call Lincoln and Teague."

"Want me to?" I put my hands in my pockets. I didn't know what to tell them, but if she wanted her brothers, I'd make it happen.

"Here's the ballroom." Olivia opened one of the double doors behind her. "It might be more private for your call."

"Thank you." Beau twirled her phone in her hand.

"I've set up refreshments, but if there's anything else you need, let me know."

Beau peeked inside the room. "Looks perfect."

"I'll leave you to it."

The door had barely clicked shut when Beau had her phone to her ear. "Can you come to West 56th?" She nodded at whatever one of her brothers said. "Bring Teague too."

There was a sitting area set up more like a living room than the usual tables and chairs in a space like this. Nearby was a water pitcher and a platter with fruits and cheeses.

Beau poured a glass of water and offered it to me. I declined and she downed it in one swallow.

I squeezed her shoulders. "You wouldn't want to do this if it wasn't important."

The doors opened. A guy walked in carrying two cases of equipment, followed by a woman looking like she'd just walked out of a department store. Her hair barely moved as she walked.

And then it occurred to me Beau was casual in a pair of worn jeans and a light sweater. She wasn't in the armor she had to wear for her father and the rest of the world. I did like those dresses and heels, but I'd take her this way any day. She felt a little less out of reach.

"Miss Hollingsworth. It's lovely to see you again." The woman sashayed over like a lion who'd just caught dinner.

If Beau was intimidated, she didn't show it.

"Veronica." She held out both hands and kissed her cheeks. "It's Calhoun. And how many times do I have to tell you to call me Beau?"

The woman's eyes widened a fraction as they flicked over to me. "It sounds as if we have lots to discuss, Beau."

"This is Veronica Espisito. A journalist with *New York News*."

A journalist? I'd said I was up for anything she needed, but I wasn't sure I was up to this task.

"Veronica, this is my husband Garrett Calhoun. Everybody calls him Cal."

There was possession in Beau's tone. She'd started calling me Garrett more often. It was still hers and hers alone.

I extended a hand. "Pleasure."

"Likewise," she said as she shook. "I have to admit, I was intrigued by your phone call. Usually I'm the one having to chase you down." For the first time, the woman's smile was genuine.

"I admire the pieces you've done to spotlight women. You haven't been shy about the good and the ugly. I want someone to showcase the truth and I believe you're the person to do it."

I placed a hand on the small of Beau's back, but it was more for me than her. What was this about? I had a slight idea, though it seemed a stretch. Some things were too personal to share.

"I appreciate that." She glanced back at the sitting area. "The hotel did a lovely job with the setup. It'll take us a few minutes to get our equipment ready." Then she tilted her head. "We might need to move the chairs closer to the windows for some natural light."

"Tell me where you want them," I said, though I was really speaking to Beau. Her show.

"I like the middle windows. What about you?" she asked Veronica, but there was no room to question her choice.

"That's perfect. Stan, will you help Cal move the sofa, please?"

He dropped his case and grabbed one end. We easily set it where directed, along with the other chair and coffee table.

"My brothers are on their way. I'd like to wait for them."

"You are full of surprises," Veronica said. "We have a few more things to get out of the van anyway."

"That's fine. And please, help yourselves to the refreshments." Beau gestured toward the table.

This was the Beau that came from refined wealth. The version who knew how to handle reporters and everyone else with confidence and ease.

"Excuse me a minute." Beau disappeared from the ballroom.

I looked around the room; it was opulent yet had a welcoming feel. It wasn't stuffy or pretentious. But I couldn't relax.

I offered to help Stan set up when he and Veronica returned with another load. As I held a light while he affixed the stand, I nearly dropped it.

Beau returned.

And she'd removed the makeup from her face.

CHAPTER TWENTY-NINE

BEAU

VERONICA GASPED when she caught sight of my forehead.

To her credit, she recovered quickly.

The bruise was an ugly purple and yellow.

But it was the truth.

And that was what I wanted the world to see.

The doors opened behind me, Teague and Lincoln nearly knocking me over when they barreled in.

They took one look at the camera and my bare face and all that stared at me was concern.

"What's Veronica Espisito doing here?" Lincoln asked.

He despised the press because he hated any kind of personal attention. But he was wealthy and handsome. A perfect combination for those greedy for information.

"I asked her to come," I said. "I have a story to tell, and I need your support."

Teague slung an arm around my shoulders. "You don't have to do this."

"Yes, I do. How many women out there are mentally and physically abused but terrified to speak up? I want them to know they aren't alone. That they can find the courage to stop the abuse."

I'd allowed my father to manipulate me all my life because deep down I thought somehow that would make him love me. It was ridiculous and stupid, but it was true. There was someone else who was experiencing the same thing. If I told my story and it inspired one person to break free, it would be worth it.

This wasn't about exposing my father or Alex.

I was the vice president of an international company. I wasn't a weak person. But I'd allowed someone else to control me out of fear that I'd be left with no parent at all.

When I'd been across an ocean, outside of my father's immediate reach, I'd flourished. Yes, I'd done what he asked of me, but I'd had the illusion of some freedom. I'd taken it and run with it. I'd gone after what I wanted. Been bold and brave. Blissfully unaware that I'd been followed the whole time I was there. Watched. But I'd felt free. Autonomous.

The second I'd set foot back in New York, back in his presence, I'd allowed him to steal that from me. I'd become the prisoner I'd been before when I'd lived in his house, trying to remain invisible so as not to upset him, yet wanting to be seen so he could tell me about my mother and just be my dad.

Some things were not meant to be.

That was a harsh reality to accept. It had taken a knock on the head to truly realize things with my father would never change. I had made a valiant effort, but any father who could let someone physically abuse his daughter wasn't capable of love. Not the kind I wanted.

"We're ready to begin when you are," Veronica gestured toward the sitting area.

I took a seat next to Cal. Lincoln and Teague sank down on my other side.

"We're clear that no video or print that I have not approved will be distributed. If one comma is edited and I'm not notified, you and your publication will be held liable." I held out my phone with the agreement Zegas had drafted.

"Understood." Veronica signed with her finger. "You are okay with the entirety of the interview being recorded on video and audio?"

I stuffed the phone under my thigh. "That's fine."

She nodded at Stan. He peered at one of the cameras, held up his finger, and adjusted the light. He repeated the process with the camera focused on Veronica.

After he had the lighting and sound to his liking, Veronica straightened in her chair and put on the serious journalist face I'd seen on television many times.

"It's not often I get a call from one of the most recognized women in the world. She's a vice president of her family's organization. She's known for her charitable work and impeccable style. She's respected not only in the city of New York, but globally. And she has a story to tell." She paused dramatically. "It wasn't what I expected. And neither will you."

She focused on me. "Normally when I interview someone, this is the part where we get to know you. The surface level things before we dive deep. I don't think that's what you want."

"No," I said quietly. "My accomplishments aren't why I'm here."

Cal threaded his fingers with mine in silent support.

"Why did you reach out to me?"

I had to give Veronica credit. She had concerned reporter down well.

"Because I've been physically and mentally abused for a long time and I didn't say anything. I want others in my position to know that staying silent is never the best option."

What if Alex had done this to someone else because I hadn't had the courage to turn him in to the police? What if she was alone and hurting and . . . helpless?

"I don't want to be helpless anymore," I whispered.

Lincoln put an arm around me and Teague reached over him to touch my knee.

"You have a lot of support," Veronica observed.

"Yet I still said nothing."

I stuffed down the shame that threatened to silence me once more.

"If a friend had come to me facing the exact situation I was in, I would've known what to do. It might not have been easy, but I would've been decisive and strong." I lifted my chin and straightened my shoulders. "Instead, I behaved in a way I normally never would. Because of fear."

There was more than sympathy in Veronica's eyes. Understanding. In a way that only people who had been in similar circumstances could share.

"What brought you out of that fear?"

I pointed to my forehead. "I literally had my head bashed into a door."

Her eyes widened at my candor, but she kept her composure. "How long did you suffer this type of abuse?"

"Physically, only a couple of weeks. It started with a squeeze of the hand, just hard enough not to break it. Interestingly enough, I didn't tolerate that." I had a small satisfaction as I recalled stabbing the top of Alex's hand with a fork. Strangely enough, I think he liked it on some level. "The next time it happened, it was more aggressive. I was so stunned, I froze."

"You kneed that son of a bitch in the balls," Garrett growled in my ear.

It was no consolation. I was embarrassed I'd ever let it get that far. I shuddered, still able to taste the stale whiskey on Alex's breath.

"If you need a minute . . ." Veronica said.

"No." I refocused on my mission. "That time I had a bruised jaw." I pointed where the evidence was fading. "A nearly broken arm, and he'd forced himself on me. I'd never felt so powerless."

Lincoln bolted to his feet. He covered his face with his hand. "*Shit.*"

He'd already heard this once, and it was no easier the second time. That was one reason I never wanted to tell them. Because it hurt them.

The camera followed Lincoln. I wanted to stand between it and him. Tell them to stop filming. But this was real. This was what abuse did to families. And maybe if someone saw this, they might recognize it and be able to get help.

"Lincoln."

He refused to look at me. "I'm supposed to be the barrier between you and him."

"You shouldn't have to be."

That responsibility should have never fallen on my brothers. Our father should have been our protection. Instead, he was the monster inside.

Veronica allowed us to have a moment to catch our breath. Lincoln sat back down, but he was like a bomb ready to detonate at any second.

"I ask this of every person I interview who has suffered repeated abuse, so please take the question for what it is. Why did you keep going back?"

"I didn't," I blurted. "I never intended to see him again or at least never be alone, especially after he became more violent. But the last time, which was the worst, I was blindsided." I touched both of my brothers' legs and squeezed Cal's hand. "We all were."

I opened my mouth. Then closed it. Then opened it again. "I-I want to stress the importance of having at least one person to call in an emergency. It might be the one thing I got right. But I should've also gone to the police."

Veronica tilted her head. "Why didn't you contact the authorities?"

"I was ashamed. And my father didn't want a scandal."

She made a noncommittal noise. "Who was this person to you? A boyfriend? A colleague?"

"Neither." I took a deep breath. Somehow what I had to say was harder than anything else I'd admitted. "Our mental abuse started when we were children, by our father. The person who physically abused me was the man he tried to force me to marry."

Her lips parted.

No one knew the Hollingsworths' nasty little secret. We weren't the perfect family. Our father was a tyrant.

And it was time to end his reign of terror.

CHAPTER THIRTY

CAL

"I'M SO DAMN proud of you."

Beau had told her story in a relatable way. She hadn't held back. There wasn't a question she didn't answer for over two hours.

I hadn't known what to make of Veronica Espisito initially, but even she'd wiped her eyes a few times.

"I just hope it helps someone."

"It will."

Until Beau had opened up, I hadn't understood why she had anything to do with her father. Other than he was her family and a person was supposed to stick by them no matter what.

I'd made plenty of mistakes, just like all my brothers. That didn't mean we gave up on each other.

But I couldn't imagine having an entire life of this push and pull. Moments of what looked like a form of love or much-wanted attention along with absolute control. It was all she'd known.

Of course it had felt wrong, but it was compounded by the fact he was the only parent she had left. Walking away from that wouldn't be easy for anyone.

She hadn't wanted to cut him out. She'd wanted to fight for a relationship with him. He held all the secrets to her mother. And he was her father.

She'd held out hope he'd change.

He hadn't.

"I'd like to go for a walk." She grabbed two leashes.

Copper and Brutus trotted over, knowing they were for them.

"I think we've been adopted." I accepted the leash she held out to me, and I bent to loop it around Copper.

"Can we have pets at our apartment?"

Our apartment.

Slowly, I straightened. "Mrs. Peters pretends she doesn't have a cat, but nobody turns her in."

"It would be impossible to be low key, especially when the puppies get older."

I gulped. "The puppies?"

"We can't separate Copper and Brutus from them," Beau said as if I'd insinuated we were going to let them free in Central Park.

Copper blinked up at me and whined. Brutus grunted at me.

I patted both of their heads. "Nobody is taking your puppies."

I had no idea what we were going to do with that many—I'd lost count of how many there were—but I wasn't going to be the one to separate that family.

Beau tried to coax Brutus out the front door, but he wouldn't go until he was sure Copper was coming. Miss Adeline was right. He was protective.

"Do you feel any better?" I asked once we were in the elevator.

She sagged against the back wall. "Not like I thought I would. It-it's all still there."

"One day at a time."

"I'm glad you were there." She lolled her head toward me.

"I'm glad you let me be there."

It hadn't been easy watching her relive the nightmare of the past few weeks . . . beyond that, really. I'd tried my hardest to keep it together for her, though I'd wanted to turn over every piece of furniture in that room and break it into pieces.

"Don't get all crazy on me." That was never a good way for a sentence to start. "But if we can't have dogs in your apartment, we need to find somewhere else. I was thinking close to your mom."

Everything in me recoiled. "We just figured out about the dogs so that was some fast thinking."

"I said don't get all crazy." She rolled her eyes as we exited the elevator.

"You know how I feel about your money." The tentacles of control around my temper slowly loosened.

"*Our* money," she corrected. "If it's such a big deal, we'll give it all away."

She strode past the doorman with a wave, while I struggled to keep up.

"No. You earned it."

"I can earn more. Is that going to be a problem?" She leveled me with a look when we stopped at a crosswalk.

Was I that guy? Jealous that my wife earned more than me?

No. I was proud of her. Impressed. Actually, blown away. She ran a major company, which was more than I could ever do, and made it look easy.

"Pop taught me to take care of my family," I said, as a little slash of hurt carved into my chest at the thought of him.

She softened. "I'm good at real estate. I can find us the right place if you'll help me. And we can finance it. I'll make half the payment and you make half the payment. Like partners."

She was trying to find middle ground. Was I willing to meet her there?

"Is this compromise? Because it sure sounds a lot like it," I said.

She bumped me. "I'm not the one who has issues with it."

"How am I supposed to argue with that?" I bumped her back as we entered the park. "You'd really live near Ma?"

She nodded. "I'd love to. Our kids deserve to live near their grandma."

I tripped. "Kids?"

"Since they'll have you for a dad, I want lots of them."

I swallowed hard. Was I ready for that? That was the thing about being older. I had enough wisdom to consider decisions like that carefully. When I was younger, I would've jumped in without really weighing the possible consequences.

But the image was already forming in my mind. A house like I'd grown up in with a bunch of boys driving us nuts.

Since they'll have you for a dad...

How had I skipped over that? She thought I'd be a good dad. I wanted to be. But I wanted to be a good husband too.

Damn it.

A nearby flower cart was a not-so-gentle reminder from Pop. I hurried over, picked the brightest single flower they had, and held it out to her.

She blushed and smiled shyly. The flower made her happy. It was a simple nothing, yet it made her smile. No wonder Pop always did that for Ma.

"I forgot the flowers earlier," I said.

"I'm glad you did. I like this one." She buried her nose in the bloom and inhaled. "I might try to garden in our backyard."

The picture became clearer. "You gonna do that in high heels?"

"If I feel like it," she said haughtily.

I laughed. We were going to do this. We were going to build a life. It would be messy and chaotic, but perfect.

Beau froze, all the color draining from her face. I'd been so lost in my head, I hadn't noticed the approaching figure.

Brutus went into a defensive posture, as did I.

"I can fix this drastic mistake you've made, my dear daughter. It's going to take some doing, but it will be fixed."

CHAPTER THIRTY-ONE

BEAU

"I'M NOT the one who's made mistakes."

My voice wasn't as strong as I'd wanted it to be. I shook with an anger infused with the frisson of fear that always came when I was near my father.

How dare he approach us after what he did? What he allowed.

He sighed. "It's not the time to be willful."

"It wasn't the time for you to set me up to have my head slammed into a door either." I motioned to my very clearly bruised forehead.

Maybe that interview had been good for me. It was time to practice what I preached. I'd had enough of him a long time ago.

Part of me was sad as I looked at him. I'd given him every chance to have a decent relationship. I hadn't asked for daily chats or giggles and smiles. Just to be nice occasionally.

But that opportunity had passed.

He flinched. "I've seen to that."

"It never should've happened," I yelled.

Garrett edged closer to me. I loved him for his support. Loved that he let me do things my way, reminding me he was there when I needed him.

Father looked around before sending me a chastising glare for causing a scene. If he'd cared that much about what I thought, he'd have gone with me to the police station to have Alex prosecuted.

"I told you—"

"Yeah, yeah. You've seen to it," I said, unimpressed.

"I won't tolerate such disrespect."

"We're on the same page, *Daddy*. Because I'm not tolerating such disrespect either."

I moved around him. My husband and our dogs were having a nice walk in the park. I'd let my father take too much of our joy already. He wouldn't ruin this.

"I'm ready to talk about your mother."

Damn him.

Damn his manipulations. Damn him for knowing what motivated me. Damn him for using her to get to me.

"But not until this problem is rectified. What were you thinking, marrying this riffraff?"

I whirled back around. "If you cared anything about Lincoln, Teague, Mom, or me you wouldn't use her to force your hand. I want to know everything about her. It's not a secret. But I'm not sacrificing a future with the greatest man I've ever known."

I turned back around and linked my arm through Garrett's, still holding the pretty flower. He was kind and decent and loving. Everything I'd ever wanted.

"I warned you to stay away from my daughter."

Garrett tensed.

"I must admit you fooled me. You did for a very long time. Now I have to get involved to clean up the mess you've both made."

Fooled him? For a long time?

I looked at Garrett, who stared straight ahead with his jaw locked.

I was going to get whiplash, but I turned around again. "You've lost your entire family and you're too blind to see it. Wake up. When nobody cares what you think, you don't have any power anymore."

"The three of you will always be my children."

"Then why didn't you act like a dad?" My eyes stung. *Don't cry. Not now. Not in front of him.*

"I always act in your best interest." His nostrils flared. "The situation with Davenport went awry."

"He almost raped me. That's more than awry," I said softly.

"He won't lay another finger on you." His tone had a dangerous quality that made me shiver.

"I know. Because he's going to be in jail for a very long time."

"That's not good enough for him," he mumbled.

"Goodbye, Mr. Hollingsworth. I tried. I really did. But you chose not to have a daughter. *Not* me." I wouldn't dignify him with the honor of Father. Not when that would put him in the same caliber as what Garrett and my brothers would be one day.

A flash of pain streaked across his face, but it was gone so fast, I wasn't sure I'd really seen it. He didn't get to be hurt. Not after everything he'd done.

I shook as the shackles that tethered me to that man splintered. I wouldn't see him again.

I didn't want to feel the hurt that moved its way through me. But it was there.

I will never do this to my children.

This time when I turned around, there was an air of finality. It weighed heavily, but with time, I was confident it would be lighter.

"I loved her."

His voice held the most wretched quality.

I held tight to Cal. I couldn't fall for this. Wouldn't succumb to one of his tactics.

"The day you were born, she made me promise to teach you how to take care of yourself. To always be there. And I kept that promise."

My eyes flooded to the point I couldn't see. Why hadn't he ever told me that before?

"She was the only thing that ever made me a decent man until she gave me the three of you."

My shoulders shook as a sob escaped. Truth and lies. This was what he did. I believed him but I didn't.

Garrett put an arm around me. There was so much noise in my head I couldn't think straight.

Mind games.

My father lost me, so he had to try to gain the upper hand again.

Brutus licked my hand at the same time Garrett kissed the top of my head.

I was loved. So much so that it was bursting from the seams.

And I believed with all my heart my mother had given me that gift.

And that was why I didn't need any of the lies Samuel Hollingsworth would spout off at me. Perhaps that was true freedom.

CHAPTER THIRTY-TWO

CAL

"WHAT WAS HE TALKING ABOUT?"

Beau drew circles on my stomach.

I held her close as we lay in the dark, still shell-shocked from the entire encounter with her father. As much as I despised the man, I'd heard the torment in his voice.

I didn't want to, but I believed him.

That he'd loved his wife. That he realized what good kids he had.

I didn't want to answer her question.

ONE MORE SHIFT.

Then I was taking Beau to meet Ma. Neither of them knew it yet, but it was past time. I'd been working hard, even managed to save a little.

It might not be much, but maybe it was enough for a bigger apartment.

Or a ring.

She deserved more than what I could give her, more than being the wife of a fireman. But I couldn't let her go. Didn't want to.

Beau was the best thing that ever happened to me.

We'd figure out a way to tell her family. And if they wouldn't accept us, mine would.

I hiked my bag over my shoulder as I strode toward the station.

I didn't want her to lose her family. She loved them. I couldn't ask her to sacrifice them for me.

It wouldn't come to that. I wouldn't let it.

A dark Mercedes rolled to a stop beside me. The window hummed as it lowered.

The car was familiar. I couldn't place where I'd seen it before, but I had.

A hard face came into view. He wasn't from around here. What I could see of his suit looked too expensive. And there was just something about him . . . something my instincts said to get the hell away from.

"You're quite taken with Beau."

I stopped, all the hairs on the back of my neck raised like they did before I went into a four-alarm fire.

"It's been good for her to see a different side of life. Why do little girls always want to see if the grass is greener?" *he mused as if she were a disobedient child instead of a grown woman.*

You called her a little girl when you met her.

But she wasn't.

I'd meant it as a warning. We'd had no business being together. She was my friend's sister and from a completely different world.

Turned out we had no business being apart.

I stared at him, silent. What did he want me to say?

"She is destined for great things. Wouldn't you agree?"

It was like asking if Ma's cake was the best. Yeah. It was. And yeah, Beau was going to do anything and everything she wanted.

He didn't wait for a reply. "It's going to be difficult for her to do that in the Bronx on a fireman's salary, isn't it?" *He flashed a wry smile.* "That is, if she doesn't grow tired of you. Riding around in that truck is bound to grow tiresome . . . if it hasn't already."

Who the hell did this man think he was? And how did he know so much about Beau and me?

And how did he know every single insecurity I had?

"She's graduated and has an opportunity to pursue abroad." *He appeared regretful.* "She's turned it down. You love her, do you not?"

My jaw tightened. "I don't see how that's any of your concern."

"My daughter is very much my concern."

No wonder she hardly talked about him. He was terrifying.

"When you care for someone, you have to sacrifice your own happiness for the sake of theirs. You wouldn't want to hold her back, I'm sure."

No, I wouldn't.

"You're living your dream. Shouldn't she be able to chase hers?"

The window hummed again as it rolled up. I felt his stare even though I couldn't see it behind the dark glass. Slowly, the car pulled away.

I was living my dream.

Was I keeping her from hers?

"HE CAME TO SEE ME."

I still felt like that kid glued to the sidewalk. Her father had read all my insecurities and used them to get me to do just what he wanted.

She sat up and turned on the light. Her eyes were still red-rimmed. I balled my fist.

He'd made her cry.

He was the one who should've been in tears. That idiot gave up the most important thing he'd ever had. I hoped his money was enough to keep him warm at night.

"When?" She crossed her legs and rested her hands on my chest.

"The day before I . . ." Broke up didn't feel like the right words. I'd never really left her.

"Dumped me," she said bitterly.

"I thought I was doing what was right for you. I didn't want you to give up that opportunity abroad or any of your dreams because of me."

She'd never understand my feelings, and I'd never be able to make her see.

"Opportunity abroad?" Her brow furrowed.

"He said you'd turned one down. You went to London so quickly, I always thought you'd taken it after all." And I'd hoped she was happy and had everything she wanted and more.

"I didn't turn down anything like that." She pressed her fingers into my chest. "I begged him to let me go to London. Swore I could grow Hollingsworth Properties. I couldn't stay in the same city as you. I was too devastated."

Stab.

I'd hurt her. I knew it. But I still hated it. Maybe even more now than I had then. Back then I'd had the illusion I was doing the right thing. Now I had the hindsight to make me wonder.

But she had been destined for great things. And she'd done them.

She was also destined to do more.

"If you had stayed in New York, I don't think I could've stayed away from you either."

It was the first time I'd allowed myself to think about that, but as I said the words, I realized they were true.

"How stupid am I not to realize he was behind this?" She pressed her lips together in disgust.

"He just emphasized what I already thought. *I* made the decision."

"Would you have without that little chat?" she challenged.

"Maybe. Eventually."

"He knew the right time and he pushed." Her face turned red. "Why is he so determined to see me unhappy?"

"I'm not taking up for the guy." I held up both hands. "I swear I'm not. But I think he believes he's doing what's best for you."

She sagged. "Maybe."

"Don't hear me wrong. I think he wanted you to live a life beholden to him. Not free. But tempered. That's what's best for you . . . in his eyes."

She quirked one side of her mouth down. "You are so right. I can see that now."

"We're gonna make it."

"I know."

I opened my arm and she snuggled back beside me. Something in me settled. She was where she belonged and so was I.

"Do you want to go back to London?"

A pit formed in my stomach. I didn't want to leave my family, but I wouldn't force her to be somewhere she didn't want to be. She'd had enough of that in her life.

"No. I want to go to the Bronx."

"You could open a real estate office there," I suggested. "Because you're not working for him still, right?"

"I can't." She splayed her fingers on my stomach. "I want to talk to Lincoln about where we go from here. Working with him is one of my favorite things."

"He could run your Manhattan branch," I said, teasing.

"Hmmm. I'll have to interview him to make sure he's up to the task." She kissed my chest then grabbed her phone.

"He's just in the next room." I snickered.

"There are three houses for sale within a mile of your mom." She held up the phone.

There was a map and three listings. I clutched her a little more tightly. We were doing this. Starting our future.

"Ugh, there's no backyard." She made a face and scrolled to the next one. "Eh, maybe," she said, quickly flashing me a picture. "This one has potential."

It looked a lot like Ma's house, similar in style, but maybe a little bigger. I narrowed my eyes on the address. "That's on her street."

She held the phone up to her ear.

"What are you doing?"

"Calling the agent to set up a time to look at it tomorrow."

"It's after eleven."

She looked at me like *what's your point* then schmoozed the agent into a showing in the morning.

"Are you any good at remodeling?" She slapped her hand over her mouth. "Forget I said that. The last time I asked, you left me."

I rolled on top of her. She squeaked, and Brutus lifted his head to make sure she was okay.

I lifted her left hand and held it between our faces. "See that? It says neither of us are going anywhere."

She beamed at the ring. "I love it. Did I tell you that?"

I brushed my lips over hers. "I love you."

"Will you marry me? Again?"

Her gaze was so open and honest, I got lost for a second.

"I'll marry you as many times as you ask me."

She grinned. "This time let's invite our family."

"I'm good with that." Ma would be happy. She'd want to fuss over flowers and a reception. "I know the perfect place."

"I bet it's exactly where I have in mind."

She rolled us over so she was on top. "We should consummate this version before we move to the next one."

I planted my hands on her hips. "Not until you're healed."

She frowned and ground against me. "You're a martyr."

"I'm a concerned husband."

Her features softened. "*My* husband."

My phone vibrated on the nightstand. Peace. Just one night of peace. Was it too much to ask for?

She stretched and handed it to me.

Zegas.

CHAPTER THIRTY-THREE

CAL

"I THOUGHT you weren't going to answer."

Zegas was far too awake for me. It had been a long day.

"I started not to, but my brother is still in jail so I changed my mind."

"He's not for long," he said gleefully.

I slid up the headboard. Beau adjusted so she straddled my thighs.

I put the phone on speaker. "About time for some good news."

"The security footage from Joe's fire station the night of the blaze has been *mysteriously missing*." He spoke in a mocking tone. "I filed a petition with the judge to allow one of our independent hackers—I mean, computer experts—to examine the company's server. And what do you know?" It sounded like he beat his palm on a desk or a dashboard or something. "She found the lost video."

"And?" I stuffed down the hope that wanted to spring free. The news could go either way.

"The fire started around four a.m. Joe was in his office staring at the wall. There's no way he burned his house down." The only thing missing from Zegas's statement was the *ta-da* at the end. Smug bastard sounded so proud of himself, but if he was right, I was pretty damn impressed myself.

"Couldn't someone at the station that night have already corroborated that?"

It was impossible to imagine that any one of his guys wouldn't have stood up for him.

"The footage shows him arriving about three. No one was around. He locked himself in his office and didn't come out until six."

I tried to let out a breath of relief, but it still seemed too good to be true. "What happens now?"

"The judge reviewed the evidence. She won't hold an innocent man. He's free to go."

Beau scrambled off me and tossed my shirt onto the bed.

"I'll go get him."

I sat on the side of the bed and put my phone on the nightstand.

"Don't you want to know who did it?" Zegas taunted.

"Do you get off on this?"

"Pretty much. If your wife was like mine, you'd be this way too."

Thank God my wife was perfect. She flung my jeans at me.

"Are you sure she isn't how she is because of you?" I asked as I tugged the shirt over my head.

He snorted. "Probably."

"All right, Matlock. Who did it?" I shoved off my sweatpants and pulled on my jeans.

Beau flashed me when she stripped off her tank top, but the sight of her bare chest was quickly gone when she put on a bra. A very lacy, thin bra.

Not. Now.

How old was I? Thirteen?

I'd have to tell her later what she did to me. Beau would get a kick out of sending my libido into overdrive.

"Just tell us who set the house on fire already," she said, hopping on one leg as she put on leggings. They molded to her thighs, and I was pretty sure she'd chosen them on purpose . . . so I couldn't concentrate.

"Was it Christina?" Who else would have done it? She'd gone crazy, though it was hard to believe she'd gone *burn the house down* wacko.

"Eh. I'll meet you at the police station. Probably better not to discuss it on the phone anyway." He hung up, and if I'd been holding my phone I'd have hurled it.

"He's a tease, isn't he?"

"I was thinking the same thing about you." I lifted a brow at those long legs.

She looked down and shrugged.

Slowly, I rose and stalked toward her. "Kiss me."

She touched my cheek. "I never should've told you what that meant."

She rolled up on her toes and fused our mouths together in a slow, teasing kiss. I slid my hand under her shirt, her skin smooth against my hand. She leaned into me. I took the kiss deeper as need pulsed through me.

"We should go pick up your brother," she murmured.

I groaned.

"You won't touch me anyway," she taunted.

"Soon."

She pecked my lips. "I'm holding you to that."

CHAPTER THIRTY-FOUR

BEAU

"I APOLOGIZE for the late hour. I know you want this to air soon, but there's so much good footage it's impossible to edit. I'm trying to convince the network to give me a two-hour special."

I nearly dropped the phone on the police precinct floor.

"I suppose there are worse problems to have," I said carefully.

"I want maximum impact. Your story is so compelling. We have viewers I'm certain this is going to help."

Veronica's words were ones I wanted to hear but still had trouble believing.

One person.

I just wanted to reach one person.

Maybe that goal was too small, but I had to start somewhere.

"I'm willing to wait a little if it's better for the long-term."

"Thank you," Veronica said in a rush. "My producer wanted to see a sample of the interview. She ended up watching the entire thing. She never does that."

The pessimistic part of me wondered if that was because I'd just handed over intensely personal fodder about our family. Something no one ever had access to.

"I'll speak to you soon."

I wandered back over to Cal and Zegas. "Any word?"

"Shouldn't be too long now," Zegas said. He dropped down on a wooden bench. "I love overtime. It means I don't have to go home."

"Have you ever considered finding a new home?" I asked, slipping my arm through Cal's.

"Every single day." He put a hand to his forehead. "If only I could find an attorney good enough to help me keep everything I've earned."

"I heard that Whitley guy is pretty good," I muttered.

"Ugh. I'm not sure what's worse. Working with him or being married."

"So once Joe's out, this is done?" Cal asked gruffly, clearly and rightly preoccupied with his brother.

"Unless you want to press charges against the real assailant." He leaned forward and put his forearms on his knees.

"Won't the police move forward?" I asked.

He smirked. "They aren't going to figure this one out."

"How are you so sure you have?" Cal narrowed his gaze on the lawyer.

"Technology helps, but sometimes it comes down to old-fashioned grunt work."

"Just come out with it." Irritation vibrated off my husband.

"Our private investigator hit the streets. Money truly is what rules the world." He quirked one side of his mouth. "That and people's innate inability to keep their mouths shut."

"I seriously doubt whoever did it decided to spill their guts," I said.

"For a price, they might be convinced. In this case, you're right. He didn't." Zegas seemed determined to drag his story out for maximum dramatic effect. "All criminals eventually screw up. Technically all people do, but I suppose that's neither here nor there." He waved himself off.

"We're not paying you by the hour for this," I muttered.

"By the minute is fine with me." He smiled smugly. "One of my guys asked a neighborhood kid if he'd seen anything. Noticed he kept late hours. Kid didn't want to talk much until he offered him a little cash money. He flicked his chin behind my PI, said 'there's your guy.'"

"It's somebody from the neighborhood?" Cal asked incredulously.

Zegas focused on me. "Daddy dearest is certainly ballsy. It takes guts to station the same watch at the scene of the crime as the one who committed the crime."

My lips parted. "My father is behind this?"

I couldn't have heard right, though it wasn't out of the realm of possibility given his track record. But why? What did he have against Cal's brother?

"It would be a little difficult to make the connection, but yeah. He's behind it."

"How are you so sure the kid is telling the truth? A lot of people will say anything for money." Cal folded his arms.

"The neighbor has one of those video doorbells. The footage shows the car rolling up and a few minutes later the house is in flames. We confirmed it's the same license plate."

"Then the police should easily be able to solve this." Cal let out a frustrated breath.

"They haven't done anything more than ask around if anybody saw anything. And the neighbor doesn't want to come forward now that they know there is definitive evidence. They want to stay out of it." He lifted a shoulder and lowered it. "Now you have to decide how much shit you want to stir up. I'm game if you are."

"Why? I want to know why the hell he torched my brother's house." Cal paced in front of the bench.

"That's something only Daddy dearest knows."

"Cal, he out yet?" Bobby burst into the station.

Four other Calhoun brothers plus Mrs. Calhoun were right behind him.

"Not yet."

Cal's mother walked straight up to Zegas and cupped his face. "Are you responsible for my boy being freed?"

The lawyer looked a little scared. I loved that woman. She wasn't afraid of anybody, and she'd caught Kane Zegas completely off guard.

"Is that a good thing or a bad thing?" he asked hesitantly.

"A very good thing."

"Then yep, I'm the guy," he said smugly.

She kissed both of his cheeks. "You'll come eat once we get Joe."

"I... would love to come eat."

I wasn't sure if it was her threatening glare or the thought of going home to his wife that made him agree.

Then she kissed both of my cheeks. "That ring looks perfect on your finger." She winked.

"Thank you, Mrs. Calhoun. Garrett told me you saved it for him."

She shook my shoulders. "No more of this Mrs. Calhoun business. You'll call me Ma like the rest of the family."

A warmth spread through me. *Ma.*

I didn't want to replace my mother, but I could have more than one, couldn't I? One who looked out for me from above and one who was here?

"Okay, *Ma.*"

I hugged her hard.

She returned the embrace then held me at arm's length. "My gracious, child. What happened?" Lines formed around her eyes as she studied my forehead.

"May we talk about it later?" I'd thought about it enough for one day and was emotionally drained.

"Did my baby boy take care of this?" she asked sternly.

"He did."

"Then we can talk about it later."

A loud click sounded.

We all looked toward the reception area.

An officer escorted Joe from the back. "He's all yours." He gave Joe a playful shove.

Joe stumbled forward into his mother's waiting arms. "Are you okay?"

"Yeah, Ma. I'm okay."

Five grown men surrounded him in a giant hug. My throat closed up. This family loved hard and they weren't afraid to show it.

"It's not like that at my family gatherings." Zegas picked up his briefcase.

"Maybe one day."

He pulled me to the side. "We can't find Alex."

Maybe he won't come back.

No. I wanted him to face what he did. And I couldn't stand the thought of him doing the same thing to another woman.

"Keep looking," I finally said.

"If that's what you want."

"I think some time locked up was good for me," Joe said. He looked tired and pale and thinner than when I'd last seen him. "That lady and her kid? Any more word on them? They okay?"

Zegas stepped forward. "They aren't going to press charges. After the woman heard what you were going through, she said she understood. But she'd like you to go to counseling. I said you would."

Joe nodded. "Yeah. I'll go." He hugged his mother. "I'm sorry, Ma. So so sorry."

"When you have problems, you come to us, okay?"

"Okay."

"Then let's get you home and get something to eat. You're too thin."

Groans echoed in the lobby.

"She never says that to you." Mike elbowed Bobby, who smacked his brother in the back of the head.

"Let's go, boys."

They followed their mother and Joe out like the two of them were grand marshals in a parade.

Cal hung back.

We let Zegas wander ahead.

My husband looked tired too. Way too tired.

"You're quiet."

"I'm happy he's free."

"Me too." I traced his mouth. "So what's with the long face?"

"Just trying to figure out what the hell your father has against Joe." His jaw was tight, posture rigid.

"What if we don't find out?" I asked softly. "Are you okay with that?"

He blinked at me as he held open the door to the police station.

"I'm okay with that."

CHAPTER THIRTY-FIVE

CAL

"I'M NOT sure I'm ready for this."

I tapped her head. "I warned you."

We strolled through the park near Ma's. It wasn't too crowded for morning. We'd spent the night at Ma's in my old room. A twin bed with Beau was no hardship.

"You totally made that up."

"We'll see." I lifted a shoulder and lowered it. "What did you think of the house?"

She dragged a few steps. "I don't think it's the one. If it wasn't so close to your mom, I would've already ruled it out."

"I agree."

Wap.

An acorn bounced off my shoulder to the ground.

Beau's eyes widened. I flashed her my best *I told you so* look.

She lifted her gaze to the tree. A squirrel was brazenly sitting on a branch.

"Better move. He looks like he's getting ready to reload." I tugged on her hand.

Wap.

"He hit me with an acorn," she said incredulously before bursting into laughter.

"The last piece of Italian cake is mine," I said in victory.

She put a hand on my chest. "I'm sure I can convince you to share."

"Oh yeah? It's gonna have to be real convincing, baby sister."

She batted her lashes. "I'm up for the challenge."

I caught her by the waist and pulled her against me. An acorn landed about two feet away from us.

"He's got one hell of a throwing arm."

She snickered, then sobered. "Are you sure about that house?"

"I'm sure. We'll find the right one when we find the right one."

She poked out her bottom lip. "But I want it now."

I kissed her forehead. "Me too."

"Then how are you so calm? This is the most important property of our lives." She fisted my shirt.

I nuzzled her nose. "I'd rather have a baby than a house."

Her lips parted.

I grinned.

"If we have a baby, we need a house."

"It ain't like we don't have lots of options. Besides, it might be kind of fun to mess with our siblings. A crying baby. More dogs than we can count."

"We'll end up at your mother's."

"And she'll love it."

She put her forehead against my chest. "I never thought I'd have this."

I hooked her chin and gently lifted. "Have what?"

"You. More family than just my brothers. Dogs. Maybe kids."

It sounded simple, but those things made for a full life. One we could build on or be content with. We'd do it together, and that was what was important.

An acorn bounced behind Beau and rolled into her foot.

She looked down and flashed a wicked grin. "I'm so telling Lexie about this. Can you imagine these squirrels throwing acorns at Lincoln?"

"I wouldn't mind seeing that show."

She had that look like she'd just had an idea. "We could have a family picnic. All of us. Think your mom would cook?"

"Do we need air to breathe?"

She smacked me in the chest. "Will you start working out schedules?"

"Yeah. I'll talk to everybody." I lifted her wrist and checked her watch. "We'd better get a move on if we're going to make it on time."

"Is everywhere we go going to be a surprise? Or is this just a temporary thing?" she asked as we strolled out of the park. "Look out!"

She ducked and an acorn beaned me.

"Vicious," I muttered. "My niece's dance recital."

Her eyes lit. "We're going to a dance recital?"

"I can't tell if you're okay with that or not," I said cautiously.

"I'm better than okay with it. What are we taking her?"

"Taking her?" My brows dipped.

She groaned. "We need to get her flowers or something."

Flowers.

"I didn't know." I held both my hands up. "But Pop would have."

"You'll learn."

"UNCLE CAL!"

Nina flew at me where we were waiting in the lobby of the auditorium.

"Great job," I said as I hugged her. Then I looked at Beau. Was that what I was supposed to say? The boys were easy. Awesome tackle. Great catch. Hell of a dunk.

I didn't know what any of Nina's moves were called. Only that she was the best out there and I was proud of her.

"Thanks for coming."

Beau nudged me with the flowers.

"Oh. These are for you." I gave her the bouquet of bright flowers.

Beau pointed me in the right direction, but I'd picked them out myself.

You'll learn.

Yeah, I would.

"They're so pretty! Look, Grace." She tilted the bouquet toward her sister.

Bobby waved. "Hello. Your dad is here too."

"Hi, Daddy." She tucked herself into his side and he kissed the top of her head.

"You were spectacular."

Nina's cheeks turned pink. "Thanks."

"Hey, before we go to Ma's I have something important I want to ask you two." I motioned between Nina and Grace, then slung my arm around Beau.

"What is it?" Grace asked, ever curious.

"This is my-er-this is Beau." We hadn't mentioned we were married yet.

Two big sets of eyes peered at her. She was radiant. She wowed me, so I figured she probably impressed two young girls too.

"Hi. Nina and Grace, right?" Beau held out her fist and they bumped.

"Right," they chorused.

"She's really special to me—"

"Are you getting married, Uncle Cal?" Grace practically screeched.

"Yeah. We want you to be in the wedding. If you're not busy," I added quickly.

"Like we get special dresses and tiaras?"

"Bridesmaids don't wear tiaras," Nina said like her sister was annoying.

"You can if you want," Beau said. "Who's going to stop us?" She grinned.

"I've never been a bridesmaid. This is going to be great!" Grace jumped up and down. "Daddy, I'm going to be a princess."

"You already are, sweetheart."

"So we can put you down for a yes?" I asked as if uncertain.

"Yes!" they said unison.

"Do you girls like to shop? Because I know some fabulous places and I could use help picking out colors for the wedding."

"Shopping!" Nina shrieked.

Even Grace couldn't contain her excitement as they did a little happy dance.

A knot of apprehension formed in my stomach. Beau knew expensive places. But I wouldn't fight her about money when it came to the wedding. Especially not if she wanted to treat my nieces.

"All right, girls. You can freak out the whole way to Grandma's." Bobby herded his daughters out of the auditorium.

"Garrett? Exactly how many nieces and nephews do you have?" She appeared a little afraid of what my answer might be.

"Thirty-seven," I said with a straight face.

"You're joking. Right?"

"I'm kidding. But I'm thinking we aren't going to need many chairs at this wedding if everybody is going to stand at the altar."

It would be chaos, but I didn't care. I wanted to marry Beau again with a ceremony she deserved.

Her phone rang and she held it up. "It's Lincoln."

All the color drained from her face. Her arm fell limply to her side.

Her eyes were wide with fear when she looked at me.

"Alex Davenport washed up on the East River." She swallowed hard. "He's dead."

CHAPTER THIRTY-SIX

BEAU

ALEX IS DEAD.

"Somebody found him about an hour after your interview aired." Lincoln folded his hands on the dining table.

We'd gone to Cal's mother's for the after-recital celebration dinner, but hadn't stayed as long as we'd planned.

Lincoln and Teague felt it best we all stay secured in Teague's apartment building. The press was going to go crazy, especially after what I'd said in the interview. I'd never mentioned Alex's name, but it wasn't hard to figure out, considering our recent wedding announcement.

"There was a note on the body." Teague grimaced. "It said, 'You'll never touch her again.'"

"He did this." I pushed out of my chair and stalked to the kitchen. "In retaliation for that interview."

"I'm spending way too much time with you people." Zegas zoomed into the apartment without knocking.

What *did* he have in that briefcase?

It was like another arm, always on him.

"No need to stick around if you don't have useful information," Lincoln said.

He pulled the chair out next to my brother and sat. "I'm full of useful information."

"Like what?"

"All of you are on the list of suspects."

I squeezed my water bottle so tightly it crumpled.

"Except your spouses or potential spouses," he corrected before looking regretfully at me. "Not yours. Yours is definitely on the suspect list."

Just the way my father wanted.

"I have to say, he's pretty good at covering up crimes and I've worked with some masters." Zegas slung his briefcase on the table. "Sure. I'd love some coffee. It's going to be a long night."

"I'll make some," Lexie offered.

"Is Eric asleep?" I asked. All this constant drama couldn't be good for him. We'd tried to shield him from as much of it as we could, but the tension in the room was palpable.

"Out as soon as his head hit the pillow." She started the coffee pot then put her arm around my waist. "I feel like I haven't been there for you like I should."

I put my head on her shoulder. "You have. It's just been a blur. And somebody has to hold everything together."

"How'd the house-hunting go?"

I adored this woman. I needed a minute without stress and violence and lies and murder.

I couldn't hide my disappointment. "It's not right."

"On to the next one then."

Pepper stretched and yawned when she appeared from down the hall.

"Feel better?" Teague asked, opening his arm.

She tucked herself into his side. "A little. I'm just so tired." She looked at me. "I'm sorry I couldn't hang, Beau."

"That's okay. You have a lot of babies to take care of."

Pepper coughed and spluttered.

Teague patted her back. "You really *are* bothered by the idea of kids." There was a note of disappointment in his voice, but more than that, concern.

"It's just a lot of responsibility," she snapped. All of our eyes went wide. That wasn't like Pepper. She hung her head. "I-I didn't mean to get snippy."

"Yes, you did," Miss Adeline said. "You might as well tell them. Or if you don't want to, I will."

"Tell us what?" Now there was a hint of fear in Teague's voice. It amazed me that he could keep his cool in an emergency . . . unless it came to Pepper.

"I'm pregnant," she whispered.

He looked back and forth between her and Miss Adeline, who nodded smugly.

"And before you get your underwear in a bunch, I figured it out. You know the only way that one will tell us anything is basically by badgering her."

"I thought you were taking a nap," Pepper snapped again.

"This is going to be a long nine months," Miss Adeline said. "Either of you have any room at your house?" She frowned. "Oh wait, you're all living with us right now."

"Oh no, no, no," Pepper said, pointing at the old woman. "You wanted to be a grandma so bad, you're sticking around for the whole thing."

"I'm sticking around for the whole thing," Teague said quietly. He touched Pepper's stomach. "We really have a person in there?"

She nodded, her eyes shimmering. "I don't want to be a grouch for nine months."

"I'll still love you."

Cal and I exchanged a look. I was thrilled I was going to be an aunt. Beyond excited that my brother was going to be a father.

And maybe one day soon, Cal and I would have that joy too.

"Damn it," Lexie said.

Lincoln immediately went on alert. "What's wrong?"

"I don't want to steal your thunder or ruin your moment, but . . ."

She focused on Lincoln. "I need to borrow some overalls. We're having a baby too."

I gaped at my best friend. Then pulled her in for a hug.

"I'm going to be an aunt twice," I said, dragging her over to Pepper for a massive three-person hug.

"I better get out of here before I end up pregnant." Zegas shuddered.

"I don't think you have to worry about that." Cal smacked him on the shoulder.

I kissed Lexie's cheek and then Pepper's. And then Teague's. And then Lincoln's.

"Congratulations, Poppa," I whispered to Lincoln.

He looked a little shell-shocked as he stared at Lexie.

"Maybe I should've mentioned this in private first." She nibbled on her fingernails.

His chair scraped when he stood. In four strides he reached her.

"I just found out. Like a few minutes ago," she said as she stared up at him.

He brushed her cheek with his thumb.

Then dropped to his knees in front of her. He wrapped his arms around her waist and pressed his cheek to her stomach.

I swayed into Cal, battling the emotion threatening to spill out.

"Looks like we have some catching up to do," he said darkly in my ear.

A tingle shot through me at the promise.

"We're *so* far behind."

He pulled me closer. "Not for long."

We were in the middle of a crisis, but our family was growing and happy and so full of love I couldn't help but believe we'd beat back every demon.

Zegas's phone rang.

It disrupted the moment but didn't shatter the intensity.

He said a series uh-huhs and what-the-hells and ended the call with a fine.

Zegas twisted in his chair and lifted his eyes to the ceiling before they landed on Cal. "You're suspect number one, which we knew was coming. How the hell they matched your handwriting to that note in a matter of hours is fascinating, but we need to get ahead of this. Let's go to the police station."

"No." I stepped in front of Cal like a shield. "He didn't do this. It's not right for him to be questioned."

"How about if he goes second?" Zegas suggested smartly. "They think you might be an accomplice. One of your fingerprints was on the note."

CHAPTER THIRTY-SEVEN

CAL

"THIS IS TOTAL MALARKEY."

Beau unbuckled her seat belt when I pulled into a parking spot. We'd opted to drive ourselves—*alone*—to have a minute away from the chaos.

"Couldn't agree more."

She whipped around, her eyes flashing. "How are you so calm?"

"We're innocent. Nothing to worry about unless Zegas suddenly can only get guilty people off the hook." I jogged around the car and held her door open.

"He's a disaster without me." Patrick Whitley strode toward us. "Happy to hear your brother is free. Actually, both of your brothers. Now let's see what we can do to keep you that way."

"Can we please keep the bickering to a minimum?" I asked, rubbing my temples.

"No promises." Whitley grinned.

IN WHAT WAS ONLY MINUTES, yet felt like hours, we were in an interrogation room and it felt like the walls were closing in.

"So you're telling me you don't know the exact time of death yet, but you've matched fingerprints and a handwriting sample?" Zegas asked, looking at Whitley like *get a load of this bozo*.

It was a good—no, great—point.

"Did your clients get into an altercation with Davenport at Samuel Hollingsworth's home? That's all I'm trying to establish, Kane," the detective said, clearly running out of patience.

Beau leaned across the table and pointed at the bruise on her head that was no longer covered by makeup. "What does this look like?"

I squeezed her thigh and Zegas moved in front of her. But I didn't blame my wife for snapping. This whole thing was absurd. I couldn't say I was sorry Davenport ended up the way he did, but Beau was the one who had suffered.

"My clients have suffered greatly at the hands of this man. They've cooperated, but we're going round and round here." Whitley twirled his finger.

The detective slammed his notebook shut. "Then we'll move on to Miss Hollingsworth's brothers."

"It's Calhoun. *Mrs.* Calhoun," Beau corrected.

A surge of pride went through me at how protective of her new name she was. When she'd showed me that new identification, it had been terrifying and exhilarating. Now it made me love her all the more.

"Again, you have no time of death. If you want an accurate accounting of their whereabouts, we need that to be able to provide one." Zegas leaned back in his chair. "I know this is a high-profile case and you need to close it fast to make the department look good. But if you throw slings and arrows at my clients and damage their reputations needlessly . . ."

The man played hardball. And he wasn't afraid to go for the jugular. Which in this case, if we sued the city for defamation, meant more money for Zegas.

"Mr. Calhoun is a distinguished hero of this city." Whitley took off his glasses. "He comes from a line of men who have sacrificed their lives for New York. How is that going to look if you're trying to pin a murder on him and his wife just to close a case?"

I slouched in my seat. I wasn't a hero, though the rest of my family were.

The detective stood. "As soon as I get that time of death, you better both have an ironclad alibi." He pointed between Beau and me. "Get out of here."

"WAS THERE A PURPOSE TO THIS?" Beau fumed once we were out in the lobby. "They don't have anything."

"We insulted them a bit." Zegas seemed happy about that.

"This isn't the last you'll see of him, unless by some miracle the killer confesses." Whitley cut his eyes to me. "Which we know he won't."

"Elliott is pulling the time-stamped surveillance footage of his building now. Once we show what time you came back and what time you left the next day, it'll be a slam dunk." Zegas made a swish motion with his hand.

"You're assuming he was killed the night of the altercation," Whitley pointed out.

"What if he wasn't? We haven't been staying at Teague's every night." I plowed a hand through my hair.

"Or what if he died before we got home?" Beau asked. She looked away and cursed.

"They're thinking like lawyers now," Whitley said, somewhat proud.

"You're innocent. We'll prove it. But if the cops want information, they're going to have to work for it." Zegas bounced on his feet like he was wired and ready for more action.

"Could you subpoena the detail my father has kept on all of us? They could quite easily prove our innocence."

Zegas made a finger gun and grinned. "If it comes to it, hell yes, we will. Now go get some sleep. Or go make some more clients for me."

"Over the line, Zegas," I growled.

"I have to look out for my pocketbook. Increasing the numbers of my best clients is in my best interest." He walked backward. "I'll call you."

"Please don't," Whitley muttered under his breath. "I watched your interview." His features turned kind. "It was riveting. You should talk to Vivian about Paths of Purpose. I do some work for those ladies, and they'd really benefit from hearing your story. I think a lot of them could relate."

Beau nodded. "Teague and Pepper work closely with them too. I'll check into it."

"See you kids later."

"Is this nightmare ever going to end?" She slipped her arm around my waist.

"Our life is going to be so boring—"

"We have umpteen dogs. I don't think life is going to be boring any time soon," she said.

We walked in a comfortable silence to the car.

I stayed in the doorway once she was inside. "If your dad did . . ." I didn't want to say *murder* out loud. "I understand not wanting to go down for it. But putting the suspicion on your kids? I'll never get that."

I didn't know if he had some wires crossed or just wasn't capable of feeling or . . . I couldn't begin to explain it. But he needed to let Beau go.

She wasn't his to bother any longer.

She was mine to protect.

CHAPTER THIRTY-EIGHT

CAL

"I HAVE an errand to run after work, then I'll be home."

I shoved the key in the ignition of my truck and felt a pinch of guilt for fibbing to Beau. It wasn't a lie exactly, I just wasn't being completely forthcoming.

"I saved you some dinner." Beau lowered her voice. "Teague can't cook as good as your mother."

I chuckled. "She's tough to beat. I'll see you in a bit."

"Love you."

The words struck me in the chest. Would I ever get used to hearing them come out of her mouth?

"Love you too, baby sister."

I tossed the phone in the passenger seat. Maybe I loved her a little too much . . . if that was possible.

She'd be pissed when she found out where I was going, but I had to do this. Somebody had to end this war, and I was going to fight like hell to do it.

You sure you don't need backup, Cal?

No, I wasn't sure. But this was something I had to handle on my own.

I cranked the engine and cracked my window. Air flowed in as I gunned it out of the parking lot of the fire station.

I'd made a lot of mistakes and I'd make plenty more. But I'd never been one to go around doubting my decisions. Pick something and keep going. And if I picked wrong, I either lived with it or fixed it.

The problem was, I didn't know what the solution was. If there was a solution. In my experience as a fireman, there was always a way to remedy a situation. It might not be easy, but it was there.

Somehow all of this felt like we were on a merry-go-round that kept spinning faster and faster. At some point, it would splinter apart. The question was: what would be left?

I swung my eyes to both sides of the street. I'd driven this path more times than I could count. Everything was the same, yet I had changed.

Beau had done that.

I'd thought I could handle something strictly physical when she came back. Or maybe deep down, I'd sent that first text knowing I couldn't. Because I'd been desperate to touch her one last time. Hold her. Be with her.

In a short time, I'd become a husband, a dog owner, gained new family, and become more grateful for the one I was born in.

"I hope you're proud, Pop." I pointed to the sky. "I just want to do her right."

I was still touchy about the money situation. But I could keep making a big deal about it and cause unnecessary arguments or figure out a way to get over it.

When she'd suggested giving it all away—and she'd meant it—I realized the money was just a piece of her, no different than a dress she wore. It didn't define her. Didn't change the way she treated me or others.

I was the one who made a big deal about it. Not her.

But she and I should talk about what all that wealth meant for our kids. We'd hardly started the conversation about a family, hadn't taken any action on moving forward, but I wanted it so much.

It was as if she'd ripped a lid off a box where I'd stuffed my feelings on the subject. I'd accepted I was never going to have kids because I hadn't wanted a future like that with anyone but her.

Now that it was possible, I was going to ask Ma if I could have the dinner table someday. It was just a piece of furniture, yet it was so much more than that. I wanted our kids to have memories around it too.

Getting a little ahead of yourself, aren't you?

We weren't that young. I didn't know if we could even have kids. And if we couldn't, we'd figure it out together.

Yeah, I'd be disappointed, but I wasn't going to let it rule my life. Not like it had Joe and Christina's. Ultimately, that had torn them apart.

I wouldn't allow anything to keep me from Beau.

And she won't let anything keep her from you.

I smiled to myself. It had taken her a while to remember, but she loved me.

And that was all I'd ever wanted.

I hoped like hell where I was headed would finally set us completely free.

THE HOUSE CAME into view and I could hardly remember how I'd gotten there. I rolled to a stop and hesitated before I turned off the truck.

Is this the right move?

I had things to say. Things Samuel Hollingsworth needed to be clear on.

I cut the ignition and grabbed my phone.

The house was dark other than the lights around the front door and a few on inside.

In the night sky, I saw a familiar gray plume coming from the back of the house. The smell of smoke hit my nostrils.

I dialed emergency as I ran toward the front door. Gingerly, I touched the knob. It wasn't hot, but it wouldn't turn either.

I rattled off the address as I sprinted around the back. Naturally, there was a fence two miles high, but I scaled it and landed on the other side with a thud.

Now you're trespassing, Cal.

And her daddy would use it against me.

You could let it burn.

No. I couldn't. Pop wouldn't approve. He'd tell me to hell with trespassing and consequences and do the right thing. Get that fire out.

When I finally rounded the back of the house, flames shot out from the corner. Whoa. It was way worse than I thought.

Glass shattered as heat burst through another window.

I scanned for a way in. The smoke burned my eyes but once I pushed through it, I found the other end of the house wasn't on fire.

I kicked open a set of French doors away from the blaze.

"Fire department. Anybody in here?" I yelled from what appeared to be the living room. The lamp illuminated on an end table had an odd yellowish glow filtered by the smoke.

Shit. I needed a mask.

Just check for anybody and get out.

I could do that. The fire wasn't too bad yet.

I edged closer to the blaze and squinted. "Anyone here?" I called.

Sweat broke out on my forehead and beaded along my neck. I was getting too close without gear on.

It wouldn't be such a bad thing if he died.

I kicked the thought out of my head. This was what I was born to do. I'd come to this house to get Samuel Hollingsworth out of our lives, but not in a body bag.

I forced myself not to rub my eyes. I pulled my shirt over my nose, but it wasn't much of a deterrent. Smoke filtered up my nostrils, and I coughed.

I squinted.

Is that . . .

I hurried closer to the blaze. There was a lump on the floor. It could be anything, but it sure looked like someone.

I held my breath and scooped them up in my arms.

Damn. This thing is spreading fast.

The path I'd taken was now lined with fire. Flames licked up the walls. It was hot. So damn hot.

I tried to retrace my steps, headed toward the lamplight. It popped and went dark as the fire burned up the electrical.

I managed to find the back door I'd come in and gulped down fresh air. In my arms was the older man who'd answered the door the night we'd come here. He was breathing, but unconscious, his face and clothes covered in soot.

A siren wailed in the distance.

It was a relief to know my brothers-in-arms were coming.

I tried to wake the man. I took him to a distant corner of the yard and laid him on the ground. No way could I get back over that fence carrying him.

I shook his face a few times.

He coughed and spluttered and blinked at me in surprise.

"Are you okay?"

He nodded.

"Is anyone else inside?"

Silence. A stone-faced silence.

"Is Hollingsworth home?"

He stared at me with eyes that spoke of a lifetime of experience of keeping his mouth shut.

"Is he?" I asked again.

"Yes."

"Where?"

Nothing.

"I'm going back in that house to find him—"

"Why?"

The question jolted me. There was more than experience in his expression . . . there was a whole lot of hate.

"I have to."

It was who I was. Hollingsworth didn't deserve my help, but if I didn't do it, it made me like him. And I was most definitely nothing like that man.

"Help is on the way. Tell them I went in."

"He's upstairs in the study. Third door on the right."

I nodded and raced back toward the house. Half of the downstairs was consumed now. Hell, I didn't even know where the stairs were to reach the second floor. This was no small house. The only time I'd been here, I'd come in from the front.

I took one last breath of semi-fresh air and barreled back inside.

My eyes adjusted to the darkness, even as they burned. I bolted past the wall of flames as if they were lighting my path and somehow found the stairs.

I hustled up them two at a time.

The smoke had cleared a little since the fire hadn't reached this part of the house.

Third door. Third door.

It was closed, and I didn't hesitate. I threw it open.

Moonlight streamed through the windows, shining right on Samuel Hollingsworth . . . who was facedown on his desk.

CHAPTER THIRTY-NINE

BEAU

"I JUST GOT a call Dad's house is on fire."

Teague grabbed his keys off the counter.

"I'm going with you," I said, setting down my mug of tea.

"You sure?"

The last time I'd been there hadn't exactly been pleasant, but I wanted to go.

"I'm coming too." Lincoln shrugged on his suit coat and followed us to the elevator.

We were quiet on the ride down and as we loaded in Teague's truck.

I sat in the middle, always flanked by my brothers.

I should text Garrett.

I pulled out my phone and fired off a quick text.

My father's house is on fire. Gone with Teague and Lincoln to check on Winston. See you at home. xo

I waited a minute for a response, but one never came.

"How bad is it?" I asked as Teague raced through the streets.

"Burke didn't know yet." He gripped the wheel.

Lincoln stared out the window.

I wasn't sure what I felt.

In normal circumstances, it should've been fear and worry. I should've been hoping and praying everyone was okay and that we hadn't lost too much of our beloved childhood home.

Instead, there was just a weird apprehension swirling inside me.

But I wasn't alone. I felt it in my brothers too.

They had good memories there, ones I didn't have. Was it harder on them because they could remember our mother?

A few blocks away from Father's house, flames lit the night sky. Fire trucks and first responder vehicles blocked the street.

Teague rolled down the window at the perimeter the firemen had set up.

"Rivera? What are you doing here?" Teague asked. "We're out of our jurisdiction."

"They called in backup," he hesitated. "You sure you want to go in?"

"I'm sure."

Rivera stepped out of the way, and Teague maneuvered around his vehicle.

I covered my mouth when the house came fully into view. It was engulfed in flames. They shot from the top and the sides. Smoke was thick. Jets of water pelted the front, but the fire seemed to be winning.

Teague threw open the door and I scrambled out behind him.

He marched up to another fireman, one I didn't recognize. "Did they find anybody?"

The man averted his gaze. "Not yet. No one has heard from Calhoun again either."

Calhoun?

My stomach plummeted.

"Cal?" I asked, panicked.

The man furrowed his brows. "Yeah."

"Why would you expect to hear from Cal?" He was on his way home. Off duty.

"He's the one who called it in."

CHAPTER FORTY

CAL

"LET'S GET OUT OF HERE."

I didn't bother checking for a pulse as I hefted Hollingsworth over my shoulder.

He didn't move.

We had to get outside.

The hallway was filled with more smoke. If I were alone, I'd drop to the floor and crawl, but that wasn't an option.

I pulled my shirt over my nose, which didn't help much.

Crap.

From the top of the staircase, I found the bottom was almost consumed with flames. If we went down, we'd be burned. If we stayed up here, we'd die of smoke inhalation.

Think, Cal. Think.

A house like this had to have a back set of stairs or another way out.

Cough. Cough.

Hollingsworth's body shook on my shoulder. Slowly, he came to life.

His hollow eyes met mine.

"Is there another way out of here?"

He glanced at the blocked staircase.

"Put me down."

"How the hell do we get out of here?" I said through my teeth.

He went into another coughing fit. "That way." He pointed the way we'd just come.

"Won't work. Fire's too hot in that direction."

"The roof," he croaked. "There's access in there."

I pushed into the room he directed and lifted the window. "Can you climb out?"

"Yes."

I let him go first. He stumbled, but I steadied him, as he tried to stand. He held on to a chimney as I shimmied through the open window.

"What are you doing here?"

Crack. Crash.

The roof about ten feet away collapsed.

"Which way now?"

Red lights bounced off the smoky sky. The sounds of the scene of a fire that were so familiar surrounded us. Only this time I didn't have on my gear.

He looked down at the ground . . . which was an incredibly long way.

"I don't like that option," I said.

"It's the only way." It seemed like a challenge. He was willing to die if I was.

But I had way too much to live for.

"When we're out of this mess, you and I are having a chat." I climbed back in the window and ripped the linens off the bed. I hoped like hell those ropes made of sheets worked.

I thrust the sheets out the window. "Start tying."

He looked at me incredulously as I stepped back on the roof. I wasn't sure if it was because I'd told him what to do or he thought this sheet rope idea was as crazy as I did.

"You won't have my daughter."

"And neither will you." I yanked on the knot I'd formed. "You must be the dumbest man alive. Instead of appreciating your daughter, you used her." And for a moment, I actually felt sorry for him. "You missed out on the greatest opportunity of your life by not getting to know her."

He looked as if I'd slapped him. "Don't tell me about my daughter. I know her better than anyone does."

"Knowing she drank tea at seven a.m. and went to work for fifteen hours isn't knowing someone. Have you ever really talked to her? To any of your kids?" I pulled another knot tight.

"You've never been a father. You couldn't possibly understand."

"I've been a son. And the relationship I had with my pop, the one I have with Ma? It's irreplaceable. You could've filled this house with good memories." I motioned back toward the now half-gone structure. "You could've taught your grandkids your business or whatever else it is you know."

"Grandkids?" he spluttered.

"Yeah. We're gonna have lots of them. And you won't know a single one of them because you're on some quest for God knows what." I scanned for somewhere to secure the sheet. The chimney was the most sturdy option, but it was too wide. We'd have a short rope.

He sat down on the roof. "I used to come out here with her mother."

We really didn't have time for a walk down memory lane.

I tied the end of the rope onto a decorative iron railing. It was the sturdiest thing I could find . . . and I wasn't sure it was strong enough.

"You go first. I'll hold you."

"She was so wild and free. Nothing like me." He spoke to the sky like he hadn't heard me. "And then she was stolen from me. I got my revenge, but it wasn't enough."

Beau should be the one to hear this, not me.

Then he seemed to realize I was there again. "I must admit, you handle adversity well. I was certain that distraction with your brother would be too much for you. That it would take your attention off my daughter."

The fires of rage raced up from my feet and spread through my body. "You burned my brother's house down and had him charged with arson to distract me from Beau?"

Was this man for real? It had to be a joke. A sick and twisted joke.

"I couldn't have planned for the drunk driving. But I should've realized Beau had the same power over you that her mother did over me. Nothing could sever it. Not even death."

The hairs on the back of my neck stood on end.

"You will let her be. Whatever you did to Davenport, you take responsibility. And unless you are crawling on your knees, begging for forgiveness, don't you ever go near her again," I said as the anger pulsed out of me in waves.

A smile spread across his face. With the flames shooting up behind him, it was like watching the devil himself on his throne. "Perhaps you are worthy of her."

I gripped the sheet rope. "That's not for you to decide." I pointed. "Now go. We're running out of time."

A deafening crack splintered the air.

Samuel Hollingsworth disappeared into the bowels of the house as the roof beneath him gave way.

And then there was nothing beneath my feet.

CHAPTER FORTY-ONE

BEAU

"WHAT WAS THAT?"

I raced toward the house as an awful noise pierced the air. Destruction. It was the sound of destruction.

Teague caught me by the waist. "You don't know that he's in there."

I'd tried to call him no less than a hundred times. He hadn't answered.

"I got somebody!"

A fireman rushed around the side of the house, cradling someone in his arms.

Cal?

But I knew it wasn't him. Cal was too muscular. Too tall.

We hurried to the stretcher as the fireman set Winston on it carefully. He was coated in black soot.

I clutched his hand. "Are you okay?'

"I'm fine." He waved off.

"Did you see Cal?" I demanded.

"He's the one who rescued me." His voice was scratchy. "He went back inside for your father. I haven't seen him since."

"Yo!" Teague yelled. "Cal's inside. We gotta find him." He disappeared around a fire truck.

My knees went weak, but somehow I stayed upright. I couldn't stand here and do nothing.

Before I could think, I ran around the back of the house. "Garrett!" My scream seemed to be absorbed by the smoke. "Garrett!"

The side of the house with the kitchen was charred beyond recognition. I kept running, ignoring the heat that radiated from the flames that danced like it was erasing the place room by room.

"Garrett! Can you hear me?" I yelled as loudly as I could.

Lincoln and someone in a fire suit were right behind me.

"It's too dangerous back here," Lincoln said.

"Garrett!" My voice was pleading as I tried to see past the smoke for any sign of him.

"Beau?"

"Garrett!" I sprinted toward his voice.

"Beau. Get out of here. You'll be hurt."

I looked up. He was dangling from a sheet attached to an iron railing that looked ready to give way. Everything around him was gone and the fire was so close to him, there wasn't much time.

"Need backup now," Teague said into a radio. "We found Calhoun."

He'd suited up, ready to go in to find my husband. But I was too consumed with worry to be grateful.

"Can you slide down the sheet any?" Lincoln asked. "If you get closer to the ground, maybe we can catch you."

"I can try, but this thing is stretched to the max already." Cal moved one hand an inch lower. The railing creaked.

We all froze.

"Burke, bring the truck," Teague shouted into the radio.

There was a pop and another section of roof collapsed. Cal ducked from some of the falling debris.

"Garrett!"

"I'm gonna be all right, baby sister."

"How can you be so calm?"

His muscles flexed as he kept holding on. "Too much to live for."

A roar came from the side of the house. Then headlights shined in our faces.

A fire truck rolled to a stop in the backyard.

Teague ran to the side and extended the ladder. He climbed to the end and my heart thumped at a million miles an hour.

My brother offered my husband a hand.

I didn't breathe as Garrett climbed on top. He slipped but caught himself, and I swore I was going into cardiac arrest.

As soon as his feet were on the ground, I tackled him. He caught me with those strong arms.

"I thought—" I couldn't finish the sentence. I'd died a thousand deaths since we'd found out he was here.

"I'm fine." He stroked my hair as I clung to him.

He smelled like smoke and ash and home.

"Don't you dare try to leave me, Garrett Calhoun. We have plans."

"We already established I'm not going anywhere." He kissed my forehead. "And after I have a shower, I wanna hear all about these plans." He pulled back, his expression somber. "Your father . . . I tried . . . but the roof collapsed. He's gone."

I waited for the relief or grief or something. But there was nothing.

I glanced back at the ruins of the house. All the answers I'd ever wanted went down in flames with it. I'd never know.

The loss of what could've been hit me.

My mother could've lived. We could've had a million good times together. Our kids could've surfed down the stairs and made fun of the creepy portraits and been spoiled by their grandparents.

That house had so much potential.

And other than the bond I'd formed with my brothers there, it had all gone to waste.

"I hated that house," Teague said as he took off his helmet and stared at the flames.

"As did I," Lincoln said, putting his hands in his pockets.

"Me too," I agreed. *Good riddance.*

"Let's go home," Garrett said.

I nodded. "Do you know how the fire started?"

We walked with our arms wrapped around each other's waists.

"It was already on fire when I got here."

I dug my fingers into his side. "What were you doing here anyway?"

Errand? I'd say coming to this house was a little more than an errand.

"To talk to your father and end this crap once and for all."

My chest cracked. This brave and beautiful man had been ready to face the beast head-on. For me.

He motioned toward what was left of the house. "Guess someone else had other plans."

Perhaps Father finally met his match.

CHAPTER FORTY-TWO

CAL

"WE'LL TAKE THE COUCH."

I flicked my chin toward the sofa as I spoke quietly to Teague.

Winston sat at the table with a blanket around his shoulders and a mug of tea in his hands.

We were out of bedrooms for this crowd. I doubted Beau would mind sacrificing ours for this man.

"Guess there's not much reason for everyone to keep hanging here now that the threat is gone." He frowned. "It's going to be kinda quiet without all of you invading our house."

"Beau and I don't have a place to go. No pets at my place." I shrugged.

He slung an arm around my shoulders. "You're welcome here as long as you like."

"Does that mean we're good? Because I'm not letting your sister go," I said.

"We're good. You love her and treat her right. I can't ask for more than that."

"What happened, Winston?" Beau touched the man's arm. She'd bounced between me and him since we'd gotten back home.

"I had a pot of soup on the stove. I must've had the gas too high..." He shook his head as if he'd made a silly mistake.

The man had cooked in that house for over forty years. He probably knew how to operate that stovetop with his eyes closed.

"Hollingsworth was passed out on the desk when I found him." In the heat of things, I hadn't thought about why. It couldn't have been smoke inhalation because it hadn't been that bad in the study.

And he hadn't moved when I'd picked him up and carried him down the hall, so I was pretty sure he wasn't asleep.

"Oh really?" Winston asked. "He was prone to naps when he thought no one would notice."

I lifted a brow.

He lifted one back.

Beau rubbed his arm. "I'm just glad you're okay."

He gave her a weak smile. "I hope all of you will be too."

"You're going to be so busy. Teague and Lincoln are having babies. Well, they're not, but—" Beau waved absently. "You know what I mean."

"For a moment, I thought we'd reached a scientific breakthrough," he said dryly. "I do hope you'll bring the children to see me."

She frowned. "You sound like you're going away."

"I'll have to make living arrangements—"

"You'll live with us," Lincoln said.

The older man's eyes widened. "Oh, I couldn't impose."

"You're the only real father we've ever had. I'm sorry we ever let that bastard keep us distant," Lincoln said sternly.

Teague put a hand on Winston's shoulder. "I know you cared about him. I'm sorry for your loss."

It seemed like something that should be said the other way around. Maybe one day the three of them would mourn, but it was likely for what Samuel Hollingsworth had never given them.

Winston's expression turned hard. "There are some things that are unforgivable."

Lines creased Teague's forehead. "But when he had his heart attack, you saved him."

"Much has happened in the time since. It could not be allowed to continue." He put an arm around Beau, and she leaned her head on his shoulder.

"Someday will you tell me about her?" she asked softly.

"It might be best if she does it herself."

Beau bolted upright.

Was her mother alive?

"I'm sorry. It's not what you think." He flashed the three of them an apologetic look. "I've collected her things in storage. But I'll be happy to supplement whatever I can that you don't discover there."

"How did you get him to let go of any of it?" she asked. From what Beau had said, her father was unnaturally attached to his wife's stuff.

"He was quite preoccupied with other things." He took a sip of the tea. "I am not defending him, but your mother's death was very difficult on him. He became consumed with protecting the three of you because she loved you so much."

I didn't miss what he'd said, and neither did Beau, judging by the disappointed look on her face. Her mother had loved them, not *him*.

"Why did he cover up who killed her?" Lincoln balled his fist on the table. "It doesn't make sense unless he had something to do with it."

"He would never have harmed your mother."

Beau didn't look so certain. Look at what he'd allowed to be done to her. "Then why not tell the whole world?"

"For him, prison was not a just punishment."

I gripped the back of the chair in front of me, glad my family didn't talk in shrouded sentences. Whatever we knew, we came out with it.

"When we were on the roof, he said he got his revenge but it wasn't enough," I said.

"Because the only satisfactory solution was to have his wife alive again . . . an impossibility." He sipped his tea again. "He blamed himself for her murder. It blinded him. He couldn't stand that he had lived and she had died."

"How did he get revenge?" Teague asked.

"He killed her murderer." Winston spoke as if he'd announced what we were having for dinner.

"How do you know?" Beau's eyes rounded.

"Because I helped him dispose of the body."

CHAPTER FORTY-THREE

BEAU

I'D BEEN BEGGING for answers my entire life.

And with every one I got, three more questions formed.

"I assume we'll keep that among friends." Winston kept that stoic look on his face, but he wasn't unfeeling.

"Who killed her?" Lincoln asked hoarsely. "Who was she?"

"A woman who was infatuated with your father. She engaged him with an appealing business deal, which he accepted. They worked closely together on it, but your father was very focused on work. He didn't notice her advances until it was too late."

Winston took a sip of tea.

"He was enraged someone would dare interfere with his marriage. Samuel wasn't an affectionate man, but he loved your mother to the point it was unhealthy." He turned wistful. "She had a way of handling him. He was a different person when he was with her."

"He had an affair?" Teague sounded as baffled as I felt.

We didn't understand our father because he'd never allowed us to. All we knew was the cold, calloused man who seemed unfeeling.

"Absolutely not. She attempted to get physical, and he went on a tirade. He immediately ended their business dealings and she lost her company." He pulled the blanket around his shoulders as if chilled. "Jealousy and rage cause actions one would not normally take."

Like murder.

"Why did you help him cover it up?" I whispered.

"Because your mother was a kind and spirited woman who brought much joy to my life as well as many others. She deserved justice, not to become tabloid fodder. Fortunately, in those days, information wasn't so accessible the second it happened. News organizations were much more willing to overlook things for a generous donation. As was the police department."

He didn't sound sorry. And when he put it that way, maybe it wasn't such a bad thing her murder remained a mystery to the public. She was long forgotten . . . except to us and the charitable contributions made in her honor.

"I always felt it wasn't my place to interfere in your upbringing. But I knew what your mother would've wanted, and Samuel wasn't giving you that. I tried in my own way to instill pieces of her in each of you." He took my hand. I didn't think he'd ever done that. "He went too far. I'd allowed that for too long. But this"—he brushed my forehead with his thumb—"and the way he attempted to sabotage all of your happiness . . . I couldn't let that stand."

I kissed his cheek and he closed his eyes, almost as if in pain.

"I regret I didn't interfere sooner."

"Don't." Lincoln placed a hand on his arm. "And you don't have to hold back with our children."

"We expect you to interfere." Teague squeezed Winston's shoulder.

His eyes glassed over. "I wrote each of you a letter when I thought I wasn't . . . I'd appreciate if you wait until my passing to read them."

"You'd better not go anywhere," I warned. "And if you don't want to live with Lincoln on Central Park, you could always move to the Bronx. When we find somewhere." I looked at Cal. He flicked his chin in a promise that we'd find our perfect house.

"Tribeca's not so bad. And as soon as all these people get out of here, we'll have plenty of room," Teague said hopefully.

"I've always wanted to experience new parts of the city. Perhaps I'll try my hand at all three locations."

Hope planted its seed deep inside me. We were no longer under Samuel Hollingsworth's dark cloud. We were free to show our feelings and love each other and be the family we were always meant to be.

Lincoln scowled at his phone when it vibrated.

"One day, I'm going to be able to block your number."

After a moment, Kane Zegas's voice came through the speaker. "With the video surveillance Elliott provided and the confirmed time of death, all of you are officially off the suspect list."

"What about the note and the fingerprints?" I demanded.

"Thanks for telling me I was on speakerphone, Hollingsworth," he muttered. "Because of the altercation, it's natural your fingerprints might be on him. As for the note, after further testing it was printed. So someone could've taken a sample of Cal's handwriting and copied it."

"And there's no chance of anyone being prosecuted?" Teague asked.

"Not unless you've done something I don't know about. If that's the case, don't tell me. Now I'm going to get some sleep."

He hung up and another weight was lifted.

"I can't believe he went so far as to copy my handwriting." Cal scrubbed his jaw.

"But you're not shocked about the murder?" I asked.

"I wanted to kill Davenport myself," he said through his teeth.

I moved to his side. "Thank you for defending me."

"I'd do anything for you."

"I assure you that scum suffered greatly for his actions."

We all stared at Winston.

"I assume we'll keep that among friends too."

"Did you . . ." I couldn't outright ask if he'd killed Alex.

"Your father did."

Like he said he would. Wow. I was stunned.

I swallowed hard. I'd never understand the man, and I wasn't sure I wanted to.

"It's weird that he's gone," I said where only Cal could hear.

"You're free, baby sister."

I'm free.

CHAPTER FORTY-FOUR

CAL

"WE MIGHT AS WELL MAKE a circle around the roof."

Bobby looked skeptically at all the people standing on both sides of the altar. All my brothers and nieces and nephews were on my side. Beau's friends from London were on hers. Miss Adeline was front and center, ready to officiate. Lexie and Pepper and Eric were to her right.

Ma and my sisters-in-law sat up front.

We'd kept it small and it was still crowded up here.

"How's my bow tie?" I asked Eric.

He gave me a thumbs-up.

I took in a deep breath. She was already my wife, but I was nervous. This time it was different. The only strings were the ones we'd attached to each other. There was no expiration date.

The rooftop door opened.

Beau stepped out in a white gown that nearly sent me to my knees. She held the bouquet of roses I'd given her, just like Pop would've wanted.

I glanced to the sky at the same time Beau did. My pop and her mom were watching down, though I had a feeling they'd been there the first time too. Maybe they'd done a little meddling to make sure we stayed married.

When we locked eyes again, I'd never felt so full. There was so much love and hope and promise. We had our forever in front of us.

She'd always been mine.

One arm linked with Teague and the other with Lincoln, they walked her down the aisle toward me. It was only fitting we got married in the place where I realized I loved her, where we'd cemented that love, and where it would grow.

"Watch out for my sister," Teague said when they approached the altar.

"Haven't stopped since the last time you said that to me."

Beau took my hands. "I still don't need a babysitter." She grinned. "Not yet anyway."

Teague and Lincoln took their places beside Beau as Miss Adeline opened the Bible.

"I'm overlooking that you didn't ask me to do this the first time," she said. "We are gathered here today to celebrate . . ."

The words became background noise. All I could focus on was Beau. It didn't matter what was ahead, we could face it together because she was by my side.

I hadn't thought much about the future. Now it was hard not to get sidetracked with runaway thoughts about the possibilities. But I wanted to savor every moment with her. Wanted her to feel my love every second of her life.

She squeezed my hands and pointed her head toward Miss Adeline, who was waiting expectantly.

"I do." Whatever vow she'd read, I committed to full-on.

"Do you take this man to be your lawfully wedded husband?"

"I do." There was no hesitation, no doubt. Beau wanted this as much as I did. "If we skip the rest, is it still legal?"

This time, I was on board with speeding this along.

"You just want to get to the kissing part," I said.

Miss Adeline beamed. "I now pronounce you husband and wife. You may kiss the bride."

I leaned forward.

Beau grabbed me by the lapels. "Don't you even think about stopping."

EPILOGUE
CAL

Three Months Later

"THIS IS IT."

Beau twirled around the living room of the old house. It was . . . not in great shape.

She hooked her arm through mine and dragged me toward the kitchen. She pointed out the dirty window. "Look at that backyard."

It was big . . . and overgrown.

"Can't you just picture family barbecues?"

I rested my chin on her shoulder, easily able to see the vision she described. "Who's going to cook?"

"Ma? Or Teague? Or maybe Winston. He makes this chocolate mousse that's to die for."

I hadn't seen Beau this excited in a long time. It was contagious.

"I thought you gave up sweets."

"Now that I'm a Calhoun, that's impossible. I've put on ten pounds since our wedding."

I kissed her neck. "And you're still the most beautiful thing I've ever laid eyes on."

She spun in my arms. "What do you think? Please tell me you feel it too."

I couldn't see anything but her. I kissed the corner of her mouth. Then her nose. Her forehead.

"Garrett." She grabbed my hand. "Let me show you the bedroom again."

I didn't move. "Don't need to see it again."

She deflated. "You hate it. I know it looks like a lot of work—"

"It *is* a lot of work."

"But where else can we find a house with this much space this close to Ma?"

I lifted a shoulder and lowered it. It had taken three months of looking at every nearby house to find the right one, and this one was the best of the bunch. As my pop would have said, it had good bones. It was ugly as hell but only a block from Ma's place. That had been Beau's priority, and I loved her all the more for it. She had certainly softened under the mothering ways of my ma. "Pretty sure we can't."

"There are eight bedrooms. It's perfect. One for us. Six for the kids. And one for Winston."

I pulled her flush against me. "Six kids, huh?"

She nodded as if it were already decided. "Six girls."

All the blood drained from my face. "Come again?"

She beamed. "*Six. Girls.*"

I could barely handle Beau. Six of her running around? I was doomed.

"You're sure this is the one?"

She glared and smacked me in the chest. "When I know, I know."

"When did you know about me?"

She groaned. "I'm still on the fence."

I dug my fingers into her hip. "Then I'd better convince you."

"A good start would be this house." She flashed a smartypants smile.

"Let's do it."

She shrieked and threw her arms around me, peppering my face with kisses. "We're going to be so happy here."

"Already am, baby sister."

She pulled back. "You didn't ask how much it is?"

I wanted to. Even in this shape, I was pretty sure I couldn't afford it and the renovations. But *we* could.

"I'm trying to be better."

She kissed me with an intensity that stole my breath every single time.

"I love you too," I murmured against her lips.

"Think you can get this renovation done in eight months?"

"That's a pretty tight time line if we're doing it ourselves—" I stopped short. "What's in eight months?"

She looked down at her stomach. I followed her gaze, then blinked at her. She nodded.

"You're a daddy."

I'm a daddy.

I picked her up then spun her around. Our laughter echoed through the dilapidated house. And I felt it, just like she did. There were a lot of years and a lot of laughs left to come here.

I'd already seen some of them as our families had merged. Ma was beside herself with two little Hollingsworth grandbabies coming along—of course she'd adopted Lincoln, Lexie, Eric, Teague, and Pepper into her welcoming arms. Even Zegas had eaten at Ma's because he was too skinny. Our family had grown, and with Aaron taking more responsibility for changing his habits and Joe in a much more stable place, I was at peace. Finally.

And soon, I'd be a daddy.

Beau kissed me when I set her back on her feet. "At least there's one thing we don't need."

"What's that?"

She looked out the window and grinned, but the only thing in view was my truck.

"A bigger car."

ENJOY THIS BOOK?

You can make a huge difference.

Reviews encourage other readers to try out a book. They are critically important to getting your favorite books in the hands of new readers.

We'd appreciate your help in spreading the word. If you could take a quick moment to leave a review on your favorite book site, we would be forever grateful. It can be as short as you like. You can do that on your favorite book retailer, Goodreads, and BookBub.

Email us (grahame@grahameclaire.com) a link to your review so we can be sure to thank you. Together, we can ensure our friends aren't left out.

Thank you so very much.

BONUS EPILOGUE

Want more of The Hollingsworths you won't find anywhere else?

By signing up for The List, you'll get this bonus epilogue, plus be the first to see cover reveals, upcoming excerpts from new releases, exclusive news, and giveaways found nowhere else.

www.grahameclaire.com/begin-bonus

BOOK STUFF

Wow.

When we started this series, we had no idea the ride we'd go on. From the first words we were sucked in and we love this family so much, we're having a hard time letting go.

Beau. She's the kind of woman you want to be friends with. Fun. Witty. No nonsense when it matters. But like us all, what goes on inside isn't always what we see on the outside. She'd be the first to say that if someone had been in her situation, she'd know exactly what to do . . . and it would have been to tell her father and Alex Davenport to jump off a very high cliff.

Like most of us, we've been in a similar situation . . . one where we know what we should do, but it's hard . . . or we just don't. Overall Beau is an optimist. Despite everything, she can't give up hope for the relationship with her father that she's seen very small glimpses of. She's also stubborn and believes she can do anything . . . including change her father.

Her lesson and journey was beyond difficult. And we love her so very much for the person she is, mistakes and all.

And where would she be without Cal?

Can we just tell you how fun it was when he first came on the pages of Crash? We didn't know him, didn't even know he existed... or that he was her person until that encounter. And we were so so curious.

We did not see Garrett Calhoun coming. At. All.

He is such a good man. Far from perfect, but he has such a good heart it completely melted ours. And some of the things he says to Beau... oh do they make our hearts pitter-patter in double time. How Beau resists him for any amount of time is beyond us!

We loved every single second of being inside his head. And are so grateful he introduced us to his family. We enjoyed how real they were. They were down to earth with their fair share of problems. And Cal was at the center of trying to hold it all together.

And we're so glad that Beau and Cal were willing to open up and share their story with us. It's been an emotional journey with highs and lows and grins and tears. We hope you experienced it all too.

There's some one else we need to address. Samuel Hollingsworth. He could possibly be the most hated character we've ever had. And rightly so. And if we're completely honest, we wanted him to change. We held out hope all the way to the end that he could explain why he'd done what he'd done and be so remorseful, he'd get on his knees and beg forgiveness.

That didn't happen.

One of us writes her best early in the morning. And the last scene where Beau and her father see each other in the park, Samuel Hollingsworth had us ugly crying at three thirty in the morning. Like couldn't get it together crying. Because we wanted him to do something to fix it. Do something to recognize the beautiful person Beau is. We guess he had more of an effect on us than we thought, just like he did all of you.

And on a very serious note... if you or someone you love has been a victim of any kind of abuse, please talk to someone. You are not alone. It is not your fault. And you are strong.

The Hollingsworths are a special family, and they have a big place in our hearts. We're so grateful that you've embraced them as your own.

xoxo,
Grahame Claire

ACKNOWLEDGMENTS

There are so many people that help along the way of the creation of a book. And we appreciate every single one of you who support us unconditionally.

That includes our families. They are there for us through everything and encourage us to keep going. They've also helped us make some seriously close deadlines by giving us the time and space we needed. We love them so so much.

We're so honored to be part of the book community . . . such a lovely and beautiful place.

Catherine Cowles, what the heck would we do without you? Adore you, lady.

Claudia Burgoa, you have been there from the beginning. We can't thank you enough for your friendship . . . and for making us laugh so much.

Emma Renshaw, you are a star. You are an inspiration.

Alessandra Torre, you always make time for us, and we will never forget that. Thank you for being there for us from way before the beginning.

Tia Louise, thank you for the light you shine in the romance world.

P. Dangelico, you've always been so honest and supportive. We can't thank you enough for that.

Marion Archer, you have transformed our stories into magic. You get us. And we love you.

Karen Lawson and Janet Hitchcock, thank you for fixing all our mistakes and making us laugh in the process.

Lori Sabin, thank you for that perfect polish you put on our books.

Jenn Watson, thank you so much for your insight and wisdom. You always have the answers we need and the perfect plan.

The Social Butterfly team, thank you for your attention to detail and helping us get our books out into the world.

SueBee, you have been one of our biggest supporters from before we were even sure we'd publish a book. Thank you for your friendship and love.

Patricia Carlisle, thank you so much for your friendship. We now have a new favorite mug.

Tracey Walters, thank you for being such a bright spot in our world. You just get us.

Wendy Ragan, you saved us from a mini-meltdown on this duet. Thank you for always being there and your help. Love you.

Belinda Graham, thank you for the lovely chats and always the chocolate. Now you just need to move closer. :)

Jessica, Christy, Diane, L. Duarte, Sonia, and Sabrina . . . your never-ending support means everything. Thank you for always being there.

And to you, the most incredible readers in the world . . . you love our words as your own. You love these characters with a passion that overwhelms us. And we are so very grateful for your unending support. We adore each and every one of you.

ALSO BY GRAHAME CLAIRE

PATHS TO LOVE SERIES

It's Not Over

Three Dates

Righting Our Wrongs

Heartbreaker

Dangerous Redemption

Thick As Thieves

———

FREE SERIES

Free Me

Trust Me

Defend Me

———

SHAKEN SERIES

Crash & Burn Duet

Crash

Burn

Rise & Fall Duet

Rise

Fall

Bend & Break Duet

Bend

Break

WRITTEN WITH CLAUDIA BURGOA

Holiday With You

Home With You

ABOUT THE AUTHOR

Grahame Claire is a *USA Today* bestselling author of contemporary romance.

A writer. A blogger. United by our love of stories and all things romance. There was definitely some insta-love. Hello? Books involved. A little courting. A lot of writing. The result . . . Grahame Claire.

Soulmates. Unashamed of our multiple book boyfriends. Especially the ones that rooted in our heads and wouldn't leave us alone. Don't worry. We'll share.

Pleased to meet you.

Our favorite thing about being an author is you, the reader. So please, reach out. If you want to get on the exclusive mailing list (trust us, you do), you can do that at www.grahameclaire.com/newsletter.

Let's chat books on Goodreads. We can gossip about our book boyfriends on Twitter at @grahamewrites, Facebook at www.facebook.com/grahamewrites, our Facebook group Grahame Claire Reader Hangout at www.facebook.com/groups/GrahameClaire-ReaderHangout, Instagram @grahameclaire, or send us an email anytime at grahame@grahameclaire.com.

Follow us on BookBub at www.bookbub.com/authors/grahame-claire

Printed in Great Britain
by Amazon